Ouida

A House Party

A Novel

Ouida

A House Party
A Novel

ISBN/EAN: 9783337032999

Printed in Europe, USA, Canada, Australia, Japan

Cover: Foto ©Andreas Hilbeck / pixelio.de

More available books at **www.hansebooks.com**

A NOVEL

BY

OUIDA,

IN ONE VOLUME.

LONDON
HURST AND BLACKETT, PUBLISHERS
13, GREAT MARLBOROUGH STREET
1887
All Rights Reserved

CHAPTER I.

IT is an August morning. It is an old English Manor-house. There is a breakfast-room hung with old gilded leather of the time of the Stuarts; it has oak furniture of the same period; it has leaded lattices, with painted glass in some of their frames, and the motto of the house in old French "*Jay bon vouloir*" emblazoned there, with the crest of a heron resting in a crown. Thence, windows open on to a green, quaint, lovely garden, which was laid out by Monsieur Beaumont when he planned the gardens of Hampton Court. There are clipped yew tree walks and arbours and fantastic forms; there are stone terraces and steps like those of Haddon, and there are peacocks which pace and perch upon them; there are beds full of all the flowers which blossomed in the England of the Stuarts, and birds dart and butterflies pass above them; there are huge old trees, cedars, lime, hornbeam: beyond the gardens there are the woods and grassy lawns of the home park.

The place is called Surrenden Court, and is one of the houses of George, Earl of Usk; his favourite house in what pastoral people call autumn, and what he calls the shooting season.

Lord Usk is a well-made man of fifty, with a good-looking face, a little spoilt by a permanent expression of irritability and impatience, which is due to the state of his liver; his eyes are good-tempered, his mouth querulous; nature meant him for a very aimable man, but the dinner-table has interfered with, and in a measure upset, the good intentions of nature: it very often does. Dorothy, his wife, who is by birth a Fitz-Charles, third daughter of the Duke of Derry, is a still pretty woman of thirty-five or six, inclined to an embonpoint which is the despair of herself and her maids; she has small features, a gay expression, and very intelligent eyes; she does not look at all a great lady, but she can be one when it is necessary. She prefers those merrier moments in life in which it is not necessary.

She and Lord Usk, then Lord Surrenden, were greatly in love when they married; sixteen years have gone by since then, and it now seems very odd to each of them that they should ever have been so.

They are not, however, bad friends, and have even, at the bottom of their hearts, a lasting regard for each other. This is saying much, as times go. When they are alone they quarrel considerably, but then they are so seldom alone. They both consider this disputatiousness the inevitable result of their respective relations. They have three sons, very pretty boys and great pickles; and two young and handsome daughters. The eldest son, Lord Surrenden, rejoices in the names of Victor Albert Augustus George, and is generally known as Boom.

They are now at breakfast in the garden-chamber; the china is old Chelsea, the silver is Queen Anne's, the roses are old-fashioned Jacquimines and real cabbage roses. There is a pleasant scent from flowers, coffee, cigarettes and newly-mown grass. There is a litter of many papers on the floor.

There is yet a fortnight before the shooting begins; Lord Usk feels that those fifteen days will be intolerable. He repents a fit of fright and economy in which he has sold his great Scotch moors and deer forest to an American capitalist; not having his own lands in Scotland any longer, pride has kept him from accepting any of the many invitations of his friends to go to them there for the Twelfth; but he has a keen dread of the ensuing fifteen days without sport.

His wife has asked her own set, but he hates her set; he does not much like his own; there is only Dulcia Waverley whom he does like, and Lady Waverley will not come till the twentieth. He feels bored, hipped, annoyed; he would like to strangle the American who has bought Achnalorrie. Achnalorrie having gone irrevocably out of his hands, represents to him for the time being the one absolutely to be desired spot upon earth. Good Heavens! he thinks, how can he have been such a fool as to sell it!

When he was George Rochfort, a boy of much promise going up to Oxford from Eton, he had a clever brain, a love of classics, and much inclination to scholarly pursuits; but he gradually lost all these tastes little by little, he could not very well have said how; and now he never hardly opens a book, and he has drifted into the odd English habit of only counting time by the seasons for killing things. There is nothing to kill just now, except rabbits, which he scorns, so he falls foul of his wife's list of people she has invited, which is lying, temptingly provocative, of course, on the breakfast-table, scribbled in pencil on a sheet of notepaper.

"Always the same thing!" he says, as he glances over it. "Always the very worst lot you could get together, and there isn't one of the husbands invited or one of the wives!"

"Of course there isn't," says Lady Usk, looking up from a Society newspaper which told her that her friends were all where they were not, and fitted all the caps of scandal on to all the wrong heads, and yet from some mysterious reason gave her amusement on account of its very blunders.

"I do think," he continues, "that nobody on earth ever had such absolutely indecent house parties as yours!"

"You always say these absurd things."

"I don't think they're absurd. Look at your list: everybody asked that he may meet somebody whom he shouldn't meet!"

"What nonsense! As if they didn't all meet everywhere every day, and as if it mattered!"

but at fifty he likes to *faire la police pour les autres.* When we are compelled to relinquish cakes and ale ourselves, we begin honestly to believe them indigestible for everybody; why should they be sold, or be made at all?

"It does matter," he repeats. "Your people are too larky, much too larky. You grow worse every year. You don't care a straw what's said about 'em so long as they please you, and you let 'em carry on till there's the devil to pay."

"They pay him; I don't; and they like it."

"I know they like it, but I don't choose you should give 'em opportunity for it."

"Oh, nonsense."

"Not nonsense at all. This house is a kind of Agapemone, a sort of Orleans Club."

place. I tell you, I don't like your people. You ask everybody who wants to meet somebody else; and it's never respectable. It's a joke at the clubs. Jack's always saying to his Jill, 'We'll get Lady Usk to ask us together,' and they do. I say it's indecent."

"But, my dear, if Jack sulks without his Jill, and if Jill's in bad form without her Jack, one must ask them together. I want people to like me and to enjoy themselves."

"Enjoy themselves! That means flirting till all's blue with somebody you'd hate if you married her."

"What does that matter so long as they're amused?"

"What an immoral woman you are, Dolly! To hear you——"

"I only mean that I don't think it matters; you know it doesn't matter; everybody's always doing it."

"If you'd only ask some of the women's husbands, some of the men's wives——"

"I couldn't do that, dear. I want people to like my house!"

"Just as I say—you're so immoral."

"No, I'm not. Nobody ever pays a bill for me, except you."

"Enviable distinction! Pay! I think I do pay! Though why you can't keep within your pin-money——"

"Pin-money means money to buy pins. I did buy two diamond pins with it last year, eight hundred guineas each."

"You ought to buy clothes."

"Clothes! What an expression. I can't buy a child's frock even; it all goes in little things, and all my own money too; wedding presents, christening presents, churches, orphanages, concerts; and it's all nonsense your grumbling about my bills to Worth and Elise and Virôt. Boom read me a passage out of his

Ovid last Easter, in which it describes the quantities of things that the Roman women had to wear and make them look pretty; a great deal more than any of us ever .have, and their whole life was spent over their toilettes, and then they had tortoise-shell steps to get down from their litters, and their dogs had jewelled collars; and liking to have things nice is nothing new, though you talk as if it were a crime and we'd invented it!"

Usk laughs a little crossly as she comes to the end of her breathless sentences. "*Naso Magister erat,*" he remarks, "might certainly be inscribed over the chamber doors of all your friends."

"I know you mean something odious. My friends are all charming people."

"I'll tell you what I do mean—that I don't like the house made a joke of in London; I'll shut it up and go abroad if the thing goes on. If a scandal's begun in town in the season it always comes down here to carry on; if there are two people fond of each other when they shouldn't be, you always ask 'em down here and make pets of 'em. As you're taking to quoting Ovid, I may as well tell you that in his time the honest women didn't do this sort of thing; they left it to the light-o'-loves under the Porticoes."

"I really don't know what I've done that I should be called an honest woman! One would think you were speaking to the housemaids! I wish you'd go and stay in somebody else's house, you always spoil things here."

"Very sorry I can't oblige you, but I like my own shooting. Three days here, three days there, three days t'other place, and expected to leave the game behind you and to say, 'thanks,' if your host gives you a few brace to take away with you—not for me if I know it, while there's a bird in the covers at my own places."

"I thought you were always bored at home?"

"Not when I'm shooting. I don't mind having the house full either, only I want you to get decenter people in it. Why, look at your list—they're all paired like animals in the ark. Here's Lady Arthur for Hugo Mountjoy, here's Iona and Madame de Caillac, here's Mrs. Curzon for Lawrence, here's Dick Wootton and Mrs. Faversham, here's the Duke and Lady Dolgelly, here's old Beaumanoir and Olive Dawlish. I say it's absolutely indecent, when you know how all these people are talked about!"

"If one waited for somebody not talked about one would have an empty house or fill it with old fogies. My dear George, haven't you ever seen that advertisement about matches which will only light on their own boxes? People in love are like those matches. If you ask the matches without the boxes, or the boxes without the matches, you won't get anything out of either."

"Ovid was born too early; he never knew this admirable illustration!"

"There's only one thing worse than inviting people without the people they care about; it is to invite them with the people they're tired of; I did that once last year. I asked Madame de Saumur and Gervase together, and then found that they had broken with each other two months before. That is the sort of blunder I do hate to make!"

"Well, nothing happened?"

"Of course nothing happened. Nobody ever shows anything. But it looks so stupid in *me*, one is always expected to know——"

bilities of a hostess! She must know all the ins and outs of her acquaintances' unlawful affections as a Prussian officer knows the French bye-roads! How simple an affair it used to be when the Victorian reign was young, and Lord and Lady So and So and Mr. and Mrs. Nobody all came to stay for a week in twos and twos as inevitably as we buy fancy pigeons in pairs!"

" You pretend to regret those days, but you know you'd be horribly bored if you had always to go out with me."

" Politeness would require me to deny, but truthfulness would compel me to assent."

" Of course it would. You don't want anybody with you who has heard all your best stories a thousand times, and knows what your doctor has told you not to eat; I don't want anybody who has seen how I look when I'm ill, and knows where my false hair is put on. It's quite natural. By the way, Boom says Ovid's ladies had perukes too, as one of them put her wig on upside down before him, and it chilled his feelings towards her; it would chill most people's. I wonder if they made them well in those days, and what they cost."

Lord Usk rises and laughs as he lights a cigar.

"I think you might have invited *some* of the ladies' husbands."

"Oh, dear, no. Why? They're all staying somewhere else."

"And your friends are never jealous, I suppose; at least, never about their own husbands?"

"I have always been told so by everybody except yourself."

"Well, I won't have any scandal in the house. Mind that."

"You'd better put that up on a placard as you have put: 'No fees allowed to the servants,' up in the hall."

"I'm sure I would with pleasure if I thought anybody would attend to it. I don't like your set, Dolly. That's the truth. I wish you'd drop nine-tenths of 'em."

"My dear George, I wish you would mind your own business, to use a very vulgar expression. Do I ever say anything when you talk nonsense in the Lords, and when you give your political pic-nics, and shout yourself hoarse to the farmers, who go away and vote against your man? Do I ever say anything when you shoot pheasants which cost you a sovereign a head for their corn, and stalk stags which cost you eighty pounds each for their keep, and lose races with horses that cost you ten thousand a year for their breeding and training? Do I ever say anything when you think that people who are hungering for the whole of your land, will be either grateful or delighted because you take ten per cent. off their rents? You know I don't. I think you ought to be allowed to ruin yourself and accelerate the revolution in any absurd way which may seem best to you. In return, pray let me manage my own house parties, and choose my own acquaintances. It is not much to ask. What! are you going away? How exactly like a man, to go away when he gets the worst of the argument."

Lord Usk has gone into the garden in a towering rage. He is a gentleman: he will quarrel with his wife all day long, but he will always stop short of swearing at her, and he feels that if he stays in

the room a moment longer he will swear
—that allusion to the Scotch stags is too
much for humanity (with a liver) to en-
dure. When Achnalorrie is sold to that
beastly American, to be twitted with what
stags used to cost! Certainly, they had
cost a great deal, and the keepers had
been bores, and the crofters had been
nuisances, and there had always been some
disease or other amongst the birds, and
he had never cared as much as some
men for deer-stalking, but still, as Achnalorrie is irrevocably gone, the thirty mile
drive over the bleak hills, and the ugly
house on the stony strathside, and the
blinding rains, and the driving snows, and
the swelling streams which the horses had
to cross as best they could, all seem unspeakably lovely to him, and the sole things
worth living for : and then his wife has
the heartlessness to twit him with the cost
of each stag.

"Women have no feeling," he growls, as he walks about the gardens. "If they think they can make a point they'll make it, let it hurt you how it may."

He strolls down between two high yew walls with his hands in his pockets, and feels injured and aggrieved. He ought to be a very happy person; he is still rich despite the troubles of the times, he has fine estates, fair rents, handsome children, and a life of continual change, and yet he is bored and doesn't like anything, and this peaceful, green garden, with its innumerable memories and its delicious, dreamful solitudes, says nothing at all to him. Is it his own fault or the fault of his world? He doesn't know. He supposes it is the fault of his liver. His father was always contented, and jolly as a sand-boy; but then in his father's time there was no grouse disease, no row about rents, no wire fencing to lame your horses, no Ground Game Bill to corrupt your farmers, no Leaseholders' Bills hanging over your London houses, no corn imported from Arkansas and California, no Joe Chamberlain. When poor Boom's turn comes how will things be? Joe Chamberlain President, perhaps, and Surrenden cut up into allotment-grounds.

He possesses two other very big places in adjacent counties, Orme Castle and Denton Abbey, but they are ponderous, vast, gorgeous, ceremonious, ugly; he detests both of them. Of Surrenden he is, on the contrary, as fond as he can be of anything except the lost Achnalorrie, and a little, cosy house that he has at Newmarket where the shadow of Lady Usk has never fallen.

He hears the noise of wheels on gravel. It comes from the other side of the house; it is his brake and his omnibus going down the avenue on their way to the nearest railway station, four miles off, to meet some of his coming guests there. Well, there'll be nothing seen of them till two o'clock at luncheon. They are all people he hates, or thinks he hates, for that best of all possible reasons, that his wife likes them. Why can't Dulcia Waverley come before the twentieth? Lady Waverley always amuses him and agrees with him. It is so pleasant to be agreed with, only when one's own people do so it makes one almost more angry than when one is contradicted. When his wife agrees with him it leaves him nothing to say. When Dulcia Waverley agrees with him it leaves him with a soothing sense of being sympathised with and appreciated. Dulcia Waverley always tells him that he might have been a greater man than Lord Salisbury if he had chosen; as he always thinks so himself, the echo of his thoughts is agreeable.

He sits down in one of the clipped yew tree arbours to light a new cigar and smoke it peaceably. A peacock goes past him drawing its beautiful train over the smooth shaven grass. A mavis is singing on a rose bough. The babble of a stream hidden under adjacent trees is pleasant on the morning silence. He doesn't notice any of it; he thinks it odiously hot, and what fools they were who clipped a yew tree into the shape of a periwig, and what a beast of a row that trout stream makes. Why don't they turn it, and send it further from the house? He's got no money to do anything, or he would have it done to-morrow.

leaves.

The boy gapes and touches his hair;
his hat being already on the ground in
sign of respect. The peacocks have been
at Surrenden ever since Warren Hastings
sent the first pair as a present to the
Lady Usk of that generation, and they
are regarded with a superstitious admiration by all the good Hampshire people
who walk in the gardens of Surrenden
or visit them on the public day. The
Surrenden peacocks are as sacred to the
neighbourhood and the workpeople as ever
was the green ibis in old Egypt.

" How long will they touch their caps or
pull their forelocks to us," thinks Lord Usk,
"though I don't see why they can reasonably
object to do it as long as we take off our
hats to Wales and say 'Sir' to him."

This political problem suggests the coming elections to his mind; the coming

elections are a disagreeable subject for meditation : why wasn't he born in his grandfather's time, when there were pocket boroughs as handy and portable as snuffboxes, and the county returned Lord Usk's nominee as a matter of course without question ?

"Well, and what good men the country got in those days," he thinks, "Fox and Hervey and Walpole and Burke, and all the rest of em ; fine orators, clever ministers, members that did the nation honour. Every great noble sent up some fine fellow with breeding and brains : bunkum and bad logic and dropped aspirates had no kind of chance to get into the House in those days. Now, even when Boom's old enough to put up himself, I daresay there'll be some biscuit baker or some pin maker sent down by the Radical Caucus or the English Land League who'll make the poor devils believe that

the Millenium's coming in with them and
leave Boom nowhere!"

The prospect was so shocking that he
throws his cigar end at the peacocks and
gets up out of the evergreen periwig.

As he does so he comes, to his absolute
amazement, face to face with his friend
Lord Brandolin.

Lord Brandolin is supposed by all the
world, or at least that large portion of it
which is interested in his movements, to
be at that moment in the forest recesses
of Lahore.

"My dear George," says Lord Brandolin in a very sweet voice, wholly unlike
the peacocks, "I venture to take you
by surprise. I have left my tub at Wey-
mouth and come on foot across country
to you. It is most unpardonable conduct,
but I have always abused your friendship."

The master of Surrenden cannot find

words of welcome warm enough to satisfy himself. He is honestly delighted. Failing Dulcia Waverley, nobody could have been so agreeable to him as Brandolin. For once a proverb is justified, "a self-invited guest is thrice welcome." He is for dragging his visitor in at once to breakfast but Brandolin resists. He has breakfasted on board his yacht ; he could not eat again before luncheon ; he likes the open air, he wishes to sit in the periwig and smoke.

"Do not let us disturb Lady Usk," he said. "I know chatelaines in the country have a thousand and one things to do before luncheon, and I know your house is full from gable to cellar."

"It will be by night," says the master of Surrenden with disgust, "and not a decent soul amongst 'em all."

"That is very sad for you," says Brandolin, with a twinkle in his handsome eyes. He is not a handsome man, but he has beautiful eyes, a patrician profile, and a look of extreme distinction; his expression is a little cynical but more amused: he is about forty years old but looks younger. He is not married, having by some miracle of good fortune or of personal dexterity contrived to elude all the efforts made for his capture. His barony is one of the oldest in England, and he would not exchange it, were it possible, for a dukedom.

"Since when have you been so in love with decency, George?" he asks, gravely.

Lord Usk laughs. "Well, you know, I thing one's own house should be proper."

"No doubt," says Lord Brandolin, still more gravely. "To do one's morality vicariously is always so agreeable. Is Lady Waverley not here? She would save a hundred Sodoms with a dozen Gomorrahs thrown in gratis."

"I thought you were in India," says his host, who does not care to pursue the subject of Lady Waverley's saintly qualifications for the salvation of cities or men.

"I went to India but it bored me. I liked it when I was twenty-four; one likes so many things when one is twenty-four, even champagne and a cotillon. How's Boom?"

"Very well; gone to his cousins in Suffolk. Sure you won't have something to eat? They can bring it here in a minute if you like out-of-doors best."

"Quite sure, thanks. What a lovely place this is. I haven't seen it for years. I don't think there's another garden so beautiful in all England. After the great dust plains and the sweltering humid heats of India, all this coolness and greenness are like Paradise."

"It's awfully hot!"

Brandolin laughs languidly.

"Hot! you ungrateful, untravelled, country squire! I should like to fasten you to a life buoy in the middle of the Red Sea. Why do Englishmen perspire in every pore the moment the thermometer's above zero in their own land, and yet stand the tropics better than any other European?"

"You know I've sold Achnalorrie?" says his host, *apropos de rien*, but to him Achnalorrie seems *apropos* of everything in creation.

Brandolin is surprised, but he does not show any surprise. "Ah! Quite right too. If we wished to please the Radicals we couldn't find any way to please them and injure ourselves equal to our insane fashion of keeping hundreds of square acres unemployed at an enormous cost, only that for a few weeks in the summer we may do to death some of the most innocent and graceful of God's creatures."

"That's just the bosh Dolly talks."

"Lady Usk is a wise politician then. Let her train Boom for his political life. I don't know which is the more utterly indefensible—our enormous Highland deer slaughter or our imbecile butchery of birds. They ought to have recorded the introduction of battue shooting into the British Isles by the Great and Good on the Albert memorial."

"One must shoot something."

"I never saw why. But 'something' honestly found by a setter in stubble, and three thousand head of game between five guns in a morning are very different things. What did they give you for Achnalorrie?"

Usk discourses of Achnalorrie with breathless eloquence as of a lover eulogising the charms of a mistress for ever lost to him.

Brandolin listens with admirable patience,

and affects to agree that the vision of the American crawling on his stomach over soaking heather in a thick fog for eight hours after a "stag of ten," is a vision of such unspeakably enviable bliss that it must harrow the innermost soul of the dispossessed lord of the soil.

"And yet, do you know," he says in conclusion. "I am such a degenerate mortal, such an unworthy 'son of a gun,' that I would actually sooner be sitting in these lovely, sunny, shady gardens, where one expects to see all Spenser's knights coming through the green shadows towards one, than I would be the buyer of Achnalorrie, even in the third week of August."

"You say so, but you don't mean it," says the seller of Achnalorrie.

"I never say what I don't mean," says Brandolin. "And I never care about Scotland."

The other smokes dejectedly, and refuses to be comforted.

"Lady Waverley isn't here?" asks Brandolin, with a certain significance. Lady Waverley alone would have the power of making the torturing vision of the American amongst the heather fade into the background of her host's reflections.

CHAPTER II.

" DOLLY is nasty about Achnalorrie," says
Lord Usk, as they at last rise and
approach the house.

" Not logical if she objects to moors on
political principles. But ladies are seldom
logical when they are as charming as Lady
Usk."

" She never likes me to enjoy anything."

" I don't think you are quite just to
her, you know ; I always tell you so."
(Brandolin remembers the sweetness with
which Dorothy Usk invites Lady Waverley
season after season.) " You are a great
grumbler, George. I know grumbling is
a Briton's privilege, provided for and
secured to him in Magna Charta, but

still, too great abuse of the privilege spoils life."

"Nobody was ever so bothered as I am." Lord Usk regards himself invariably with compassion as an ill-used man. "You always take everything lightly; but then you aren't married and I suppose you get *some* of your rents?"

"I have always been rather poor, but I don't mind it. So long as I needn't shut up or let the old place, and can keep my boat afloat, I don't much care about anything more. I've enough for myself."

"Ah, that's just it; but when one has no end of family expenses and four great houses to keep up, and the counties looking to one for everything, and the farmers, poor devils, ruined themselves, it's another matter. I assure you if I hadn't made that sacrifice of Achnalorrie——"

Lady Usk coming out of the garden-room down the steps of one of the low

windows spares Brandolin the continuation
of the lament. She looks pretty. Mind-
ful of her years, she holds a rose-lined sun
umbrella over her head, the lace and muslin
of her breakfast gown sweep the lawn
softly ; she has her two daughters with
her, the Ladies Alexandra and Hermoine,
known as Dodo and Lilie. She welcomes
Brandolin with mixed feelings, though with
unmixed suavity. She is glad to see him
because he amuses Usk, and is a person
of wit and distinction whom everybody
tries to draw to their houses ; but then he
upsets all her nicely-balanced combinations.
There is nobody for him ; he will be the
"one out" when all her people are so
nicely arranged and paired ; and as she is
aware that he is not a person to be recon-
ciled to such isolation, he will dispossess
somebody else and cause probably those
very dissensions and complications from
which it is always her effort to keep her

Brandolin makes himself charming in return, and turns pretty compliments to her and the children, which he can do honestly, for he has always liked her, and the two young girls are as agreeable objects of contemplation as youth, good looks, fair skins, pretty frocks, open air, much exercise, and an indescribable air of "breeding" can make them. An English patrician child is one of the prettiest and most wholesome things on the face of the earth.

He presently goes to play lawn tennis with them and their youngest brother Cecil, called the Babe ; and Lady Usk, under her rose-lined umbrella, sits as umpire, while her lord saunters off disconsolately to an interview with his steward. In these times those interviews are of an unbroken melancholy, and always result in producing the conviction in his mind that Great Britain cannot possibly last out another year. Without the nobility and gentry, what will she be? And they will all go to the lands they've bought in America, if they're in luck, and if they aren't will have to turn shoeblacks.

"But the new electorate won't have its shoes blacked; won't even have any shoes to black," suggests Mr. Lanyon, the land steward, who began life as an oppidan at Eton and captain of an Eight, but has been glad to take refuge from the storm on the estates of his old Eton comrade, a trust which he discharges with as much zeal as discretion, dwelling contentedly in a rose-covered grange on the edge of the home woods of Surrenden. If Boom finds things at all in order when he comes into possession it will be wholly due to John Lanyon.

In one of the pauses of their game the tennis players hear the brake and the omnibus returning. None of those whom they bring will be visible until luncheon at two o'clock.

"Have you anybody very nice, Lady Usk?" asks Brandolin of his hostess.

She hesitates; there are some women that he would call nice, but then they each have their man. "I hardly know," she answers, vaguely. "You don't like many people, if I remember——"

"All ladies, surely," says Brandolin, with due gravity.

"I'm sure you don't like Grandma Sophy," says the saucy Babe, sitting cross-legged in front of him. He means the Dowager Duchess of Derry, a very unpleasant person of strong principles, called by the profane "Sophia, by the grace of God," because she ruled Ireland in a viceroyalty of short duration and long enduring mischief. She and Brandolin do not agree, a fact which the Babe has seen and noted with the all-seeing eyes of a petted boy who is too much in his mother's drawing-rooms.

"I plead guilty to having offended Her Grace Sophia," says Brandolin, "but I conclude that Lady Usk's guests are not all like that most admirable lady."

The Babe and his sisters laugh with much irreverent enjoyment; Her Grace is not more appreciated by her grandchildren than she was by Ireland.

"If I had known you were going to be so kind as to remember us, I would have invited some of your friends," says his hostess, without coming to the rescue of her august mother's name. "I am so sorry; but there is nobody I think who will be very sympathetic to you. Besides, you know them all already."

"And is that fatal to sympathy? What a cruel suggestion, dear Lady Usk!"

"Sympathy is best new, like a glove. It fits best; you don't see any wrinkles in it for the first hour."

"What cynicism! Do you know that I am very fond of old gloves. But then, I never was a dandy——"

"Lord Brandolin will like Madame Sabaroff," says Dodo, a very *eveillé* young lady of thirteen.

"Fair prophetess, why? And who is Madame Sabaroff? A second O. K., a female Stepniak?"

"What are those?" says Dodo. "She is very handsome, and a princess in her own right."

"She gave me two Ukraine ponies and a real drochsky," says the Babe.

"And Boom a Circassian mare, all white, and each of us a set of Siberian turquoises," says Lillie.

"Her virtues must be as many as her charms," says Brandolin.

laugh."

"My tastes are Catholic where your adorable sex is in question," says Brandolin. "I am not sure that I do like fast women; they are painful to one's vanity; they flirt with everybody."

Lady Usk smiles. "The season before last I recollect——"

"Dearest lady, don't revert to prehistoric times. Nothing is so disagreeable as to think this year of what we liked last year."

"It was Lady Leamington last year!" cries the terrible Babe.

Brandolin topples him over on the grass and hoists him up on his own shoulders. "You precocious rascal! What will you be when you are twenty?"

"Babe's future is a thing of horror to

placidly.

"Who is Madame Sabaroff?" asks Brandolin again, with a vague curiosity.

"A princess in her own right; a goddaughter of the Emperor's," says Dodo. "She is so handsome, and her jewels—you never saw such jewels."

"Her father was a Prince Karounine," adds Lady Usk, "and her husband held some very high place at Court, I forget what."

"Held? Is he disgraced, then, or dead?"

"Oh! dead; that is what is so nice for her," says Dodo.

"Heartless Dodo!" says Brandolin. "Then if I marry you four years hence I must kill myself to become endeared

"She has not a grain of any human feeling, except for her dog."

Dodo laughs. She likes to be called heartless: she thinks it is *chic* and grown up; she will weep over a lame puppy, a beaten horse, a dead bird; but she is "hard as nails to humans," as her brother Boom phrases it.

"Somebody will reign some day where the Skye reigns now over Dodo's soul. Happy somebody!" says Brandolin. "I shall be too old to be that somebody. Besides, Dodo will demand from fate an Adonis and a Crœsus in one!"

Dodo smiles, showing her pretty white teeth: she likes the banter and the flirtation with some of her father's friends. She feels quite old; in four years' time her mother will present her, and she means to marry directly after that.

"When does this Russian goddess, who drops ponies and turquoises out of the clouds, arrive here?" asks Brandolin, as he picks up his racquet to resume the game.

"She won't be here for three days," says Lady Usk.

"Then I fear I shall not see her."

"Oh, nonsense. You must stay all the month, at least."

"You are too good, but I have so many engagements.

"Engagements are made to be broken. I am sure George will not let you go."

"We won't let you go," cries the Babe, dragging him off to the nets, "and I'll drive you this afternoon behind my ponies."

"I have gone through most perils that can confront a man, Babe, and I shall be equal even to that," says Brandolin.

He is a great favourite with the children at Surrenden, where he has always passed some weeks of most years ever since they can remember, or he either, for he was a godson and ward of the late Lord Usk, and always welcome there. His parents died in his infancy; even a long minority failed to make him a rich man. He has, however, as he had said, enough for his not extravagant desires, and he is able to keep his old estate of St. Hubert's Lea, in Warwickshire, unembarrassed. His chief pleasure has been travelling and sailing, and he has travelled and sailed wherever a horse or a dromedary, a schooner or a canoe, can penetrate. He has told some of his travels in books so admirably written that, *mirabile dictu!* they please both learned people and lazy people. They have earned him a reputation beyond the drawing-rooms and clubs of his own fashionable acquaintances. He has even considerable learning himself, although he carries it so lightly that few people suspect it. He has had a great many passions in his life, but they have none of them made any very profound impression on him. When any one of them has grown tiresome or seemed likely to enchain him more than he thought desirable, he has always gone to Central Asia or the South Pole. The butterflies which he has broken on his wheel have, however, been of that order which is not crushed by abandonment, but mends itself easily and soars to new spheres. He is incapable of harshness to either man or woman, and his character has a warmth, a gaiety, and a sincerity in it, which endear him inexpressibly to all his friends. His friendships have hitherto been deeper and more enduring than his amours. He is, on the whole, happy; as happy as any thinking being can be in this world of anomalies and purposeless pains.

"But then you always digest all you eat," Usk remarks to him, enviously.

"Put it the other way and be nearer
the point," says Brandolin. "I always eat
what I can digest, and I always leave off
with an appetite."

"I should be content if I could begin
with one," says Usk.

Brandolin is indeed singularly abstemious
in the pleasures of the table, to which the
good condition of his nerves and constitution may no doubt be attributed. "I have
found that eating is an almost entirely un-
necessary indulgence," he says in one of his
books. "If an Arab can ride, fight, kill
lions and slay Frenchmen on a mere handful
of pulse or of rice, why cannot we live on
it too?" Whereat Usk wrote once on the
margin of the volume in pencil, "Why
should we?"

The author seeing this one day wrote also
on the margin: "For the best of all reasons:
to do away with dyspepsia and with doctors
who keep their carriages on our indigestion

and make fifty-thousand a year each out of it."

Usk allowed that the reason was excellent; but then the renunciation involved was too enormous.

CHAPTER III.

LET it not for an instant be supposed that
the guests of Surrenden are people looked
in the least coldly or shyly on by society.
Not they. They go to Drawing-rooms,
which means nothing; they are invited to
State balls and State concerts, which means
much. They are amongst the most eminent
leaders of that world of fashion which has
of late revolutionised taste, temper and
society in England. Mrs. Wentworth
Curzon sails a little near the wind, perhaps
because she is careless, and now and then
Lady Dawlish has been "talked about,"
because she has a vast number of debts
and a lord who occasionally makes scenes,
but with these exceptions, all these ladies

are as safe on their pedestals as if they were marble statues of chastity. That their tastes are studied and their men asked to meet them everywhere is only a matter of delicate attention, like the bouquets which the housekeeper sets out in their bedrooms and the new novels which are laid on their writing tables.

The guests are numerous, they might even be said to be miscellaneous were it not that they all belong to the same set. There is Mr. Wootton, who believes himself destined to play in the last years of the nineteenth century the part played by Charles Greville in the earlier. There is Lord Vanstone, an agreeable, eccentric, unsatisfactory valetudinarian, who ought to have done great things with his life, but has always been too indolent, and had too bad health to carry out his friends' very large expectations of him. There is the young Duke of Whitby, good-natured and foolish, with a simple pleasant face and a very shy manner. "If I had that ass's opportunities I'd make the world spin," says Wriothesley Ormond, who is a very poor and a very witty member of Parliament, and also, which he values more, the most popular member of the Marlborough. There is Lord Iona, very handsome, very silent, very much sought after and spoilt by women. There is Hugo Mountjoy, a pretty young fellow in the Guards, with a big fortune and vague ideas that he ought to "do something;" he is not sure what. There is Lawrence Hamilton, who, as far as is possible in an age when men are clothed, but do not dress, gives the law to St. James-street in matters of male toilette. There is Sir Adolphus Beaumanoir, an ex-diplomatist, admirably preserved, charmingly loquacious, and an unconscionable flirt, though he is seventy. Each of these happy or unhappy beings

has the lady invited to meet him in whom
his affections are supposed to be centred,
for the time being, in those tacit but
potent relations which form so large a
portion of men and women's lives in these
days. It is this condonance on the part
of his wife which George Usk so entirely
denounces, although he would be very
much astonished and very much annoyed
if she made any kind of objections to
inviting Dulcia Waverley. Happily, there
is no Act of Parliament to compel any
of us to be consistent, or where would
anybody be?

Lady Dolgelly, much older than himself,
and with a *taille de couturière*, as all her
intimate friends delight to reveal, is supposed to be indispensable to the existence
of His Grace of Whitby: Lord Vanstone
would depart to-morrow if he did not find
here a certain Countess from the Austrian
Legation; Lady Leamington is not less

necessary to the happiness of Wriothesley Ormond. Mr. Wootton would be supposed incapable of cutting a single joke or telling a single good story unless his spirits were sustained by the presence of Mrs. Faversham, the prettiest brunette in the universe, for whom Worth is supposed to make marvellous combinations of rose and gold, of amber and violet, of deep orange and black, and of a wondrous yellow like that of the daffodil, which no one dares to wear but herself. Mrs. Wentworth Curzon is the momentary goddess of Lawrence Hamilton, and Lord Iona, as far as he has ever opened his handsome mouth to say anything "serious," has sworn himself the slave of Madame de Caillac. Sir Adolphus has spread the ægis of his semi-paternal affection over the light little head of that extravagant little beauty, Lady Dawlish, whilst Hugo Mountjoy is similarly protected by the prescient wisdom and the rare experience of his kindest of friends, Lady Arthur Audley.

"I like my house to be pleasant," says Dorothy Usk, and she does not look any further than that ; as for people's affairs, she is not supposed to know anything about them. She knows well enough that Iona would not come to her unless she had asked the Marquise de Caillac, and she is fully aware that Lawrence Hamilton would never bestow the câchet of his illustrious presence on Surrenden unless Mrs. Wentworth Curzon brought thither her *fourgons*, her maids, her collie dog, her famous emeralds, and her no less famous fans. Of course she knows that, but she is not supposed to know it. Nobody except her husband would be so ill-bred as to suggest that she did know it; and if any of her people should ever by any mischance forget their tact and stumble into the newspapers, or become notorious by any other accident, she will drop them, and nobody will be more surprised at the discovery of their naughtiness than herself. Yet, she is a kind woman, a virtuous woman, a very warm friend, and not more insincere in her friendships than anyone else ; she is only a hostess of the last lustre of the nineteenth century, a woman who knows her London and follows it in all its amazing and illimitable condonations as in its eccentric and exceptional severities. "Such an awfully jolly person, don't you know?" her young men all say of her.

These young men are all exact patterns of one another, the typical young Englishman of the last years of this curious century ; the Masher pure and simple ; close shaven, close cropped, faultlessly clothed, small of person, small of features, stiff, pale, insignificant, polite, supercilious, indifferent ; occasionally amusing, but never by any chance original ; much concerned as to health, climate, and their own nerves ; often talking of their physicians, and flitting southward before cold weather like swallows, though they have nothing whatever definite the matter with them.

These young men are all convinced that England is on the brink of ruin, and they talk of it in the same tone with which they say that their cigarette is out or the wind is in the east. The Throne, the Church, the Lords, and the Thirty-nine Articles are all going down pell-mell next week, and it is very shocking ; nevertheless, there is no reason why they should not be studious of their digestions and very anxious about the parting of their hair.

with bringing about this impending cata-
clysm. That all the grand old houses standing empty, or let to strangers, amongst the
rich Herefordshire pastures, the green
Warwickshire woods, the red Devon up-
lands, the wild Westmoreland fells, may
have also something to do with it, never
occurs to them. That while they are
flirting at Aix, wintering at Pau, throwing
comfits at Rome, losing on the red at
Monaco, touring in California or yawning in
Berlin, the demagogue's agents are whisper-
ing to the smock-frocks in the meadows,
or pouring the gall of greed and hatred
into the amber ale of the village pothouse,
never occurs to them. If anyone suggests
it, they stare : " Such a beastly climate,
you know; nobody can stand it. Live in
the country? Oh, Lord! who could live in
the country ?"

And then they wonder that Mr. George
has replaced Sir Roger de Coverley, and

that Joseph Chamberlain's voice is heard
instead of Edmund Burke's.

Their host could kick them with a sensation of considerable satisfaction. Their
neatness, smallness, and self-complacency
irritate him excessively. The bloods of
George IV.'s time at least were men—so
he says.

"You do these poor boys injustice," says
Brandolin. "When they get out in a
desert, or are left to roast and die under
the equator, they put off all their affectations
with their starched cambric, and are not
altogether unworthy of their great-grand-
fathers. Britons are still bad ones to beat
when the trial comes."

"They must leave their constitutions
at their clubs then, and their nervous
system in their hat-boxes," growls Usk.
"If you are like those namby-pamby
fellows when you are twenty, Boom, I'll
put a bullet through your head myself,"

he says to his heir one morning, when that good-looking and high-spirited boy has come back from Suffolk.

Boom laughs. He is a careless, high-spirited, extravagant lad, and he does not at present lean towards the masher type. Gordon is in his head; that is his idea of a man. The country had one hero in this century, and betrayed him, and honours his betrayer; but the hearts of the boys beat truer than that of the House of Commons and the New Electorate. They remember Gordon, with a noble, headlong, Quixotic wish to go and do likewise. That one lonely figure standing out against the yellow light of the desert, may perhaps be as a Pharos to the youth of his nation, and save them from the shipwreck which is nigh.

grandfathers made it.   I don't think they will, even if Chamberlain and Company will let them, which they certainly won't."

"Tell you what it is," says Usk, "it all comes of having second horses hunting, and loaders behind you out shooting."

" You confound cause and effect.   The race wouldn't have come to second horses and men to load if it hadn't degenerated. Second horses and men to load, indicate in England just what pasties of nightingales' tongues, and garlands of roses indicated with the Romans—effeminacy and self-indulgence. The Huns and the Goths were knocking at their doors, and Demos and the Débacle are knocking at ours.   History repeats itself, which is lamentable, for its amazing tendency to tell the same tale again and again makes it a bore."

very palm of the desert for vigour and force ; whilst the English young man gets smaller and smaller, slighter and slighter, and has the nerves of an old maid, and the habits of a valetudinarian. It is uncommonly droll, and if the disparity goes on increasing, the ladies will not only get the franchise, but they will carry the male voter to the polling-place on their shoulders."

"As the French women did their husbands out of some town that surrendered in some war," said Boom, who was addicted to historical illustration, and never lost occasion to display it.

"They won't carry their *husbands*," murmurs Brandolin. "They'll drive *them*, and carry somebody else."

"Will they have any husbands at all when they can do as they like?" says Boom.

"Probably not," says Brandolin. "My dear boy, what an earthly paradise awaits you when you shall be of mature age, and shall have seen us all descend one by one into the tomb, with all our social prejudices and antiquated ways."

"I daresay he'll be a navvy in New Guinea by that time, and all his acres here will be being let out by the State at a rack-rent which the people will call free land," says the father with a groan.

"Very possible, too," replied Brandolin.

The boy's eyes go thoughtfully towards the landscape beyond the windows, the beautiful lawns, the smiling gardens, the rolling woods. A look of resolution comes over his fair, frank face.

"They shan't take *our* lands without a fight for it," he says, with a flush on his cheeks.

"And the fight will be a fierce one," says Brandolin, with a sigh, "and I'm afraid it is in Mr. Gladstone's ' dim and distant future'—that is to say, very near at hand indeed."

"Well, I shall be ready," says the lad.
Both his father and Brandolin are silent,
vaguely touched by the look of the gallant
and gracious boy, as he stands there with
the sun in his brave blue eyes, and thinking
of the troubled time which will await his
manhood in this green old England, cursed
by the spume of wordy demagogues, and
hounded on to envenomed hatreds and
causeless discontents that the professional
politician may fatten on her woes.

What will Boom live to see?

It will be a sorry day for the country
when her wooded parks and stately houses
are numbered with the things that are no
more.

Brandolin puts his arm over the boy's
shoulder, and walks away with him a little
way under the deep boughs of yew.

"Look here, Boom," he says to him,
"you don't mean to be like those fellows,
but you don't know how hard it is to get

out of the fashion of one's set, to avoid going with the stream of one's contemporaries. Nobody can say what will be the style of the 'best men' when you're of age, but I'm much afraid it will still be the Masher. The Masher is not very vicious, he is often cultured, he is a more harmless animal than he tries to appear, but he is weak, and we are coming on times, or times are coming on us, when an English gentleman will want to be very strong if he is to hold his own and save his country from shame in her old age. Don't be conventional. Scores of people who would be ashamed to seem virtuous haven't courage to resist appearing vicious. Don't talk all that odious slang which is ruining English. Don't get into that stupid way of counting the days and seasons by steeplechases, coursing meetings, flat races, and the various different things to be shot at. Sport is all very well in its place, but

Squire Allworthy beating the turnips with a brace of setters, is a different figure to Lord Newgold sending his hampers of pheasants to Leadenhall. Certainly, Mr. Bradlaugh has no more right to make a misdemeanour of our covert-shooting, and put the axe to our home woods, than we have to make a misdemeanour of his shoes and stockings, or put an axe to his head. But I think if of our own accord we centred our minds and spent our guineas less on our preserves, we might be wiser, and if we grudged our woods less to the hawk and the woodpecker, and the owl and the jay, and all the rest of their native population, we should be wiser still. I never see a beast or a bird caught or dead in a keeper's trap but that I think to myself that after all, if we ourselves are caught in the grinning jaws of anarchy, it will really be only partial justice on our injustice. Only I fear that it won't better the birds and beasts very much ; even when we all go to prison for the crime of property, Bradlaugh will grub up their leafy haunts with a steam plough from Chicago."

CHAPTER IV.

MEANWHILE, let the country be going to the dogs as it may, Surrenden is full of very gay people, and all its more or less well-matched doves are cooing comfortably whilst the legitimate partners of their existences are diverting themselves in other scenes, Highland moors, German baths, French chateaux, Channel yachting, or other English country houses. It is George Usk's opinion that the whole thing is immoral, yet he is by no means a moral person himself. His wife, on the contrary, thinks that it is the only way to have your house liked, and that nobody is supposed to know anything, and that nothing of that sort matters; yet she is a woman who, on her own account, has never done anything that she would in the least mind having printed in the *Morning Post* to-morrow.

"Strange contradiction!" muses Brandolin. "Here is George, who's certainly no better than he should be, halloaing out for Dame Propriety, and here's my lady, who's always run as straight as a crow flies, making an Agapemone of her house to please her friends. To the pure all things are pure, I suppose, but if purity can stand Mrs. Wentworth Curzon and Lady Dawlish, I think I shall select *my* wife from amongst *les jolies impures.*"

However, he takes care audibly to hold up his hostess's opinions, and condemn her lord's.

principles, as becomes a man of the world; he is even considered by many of his friends a good deal too lax in all his views, but in the depths of his soul there is a vague dislike to similar looseness of principle in women. He may have been glad enough to avail himself of the defect; that is another matter: he does not like it, does not admire it; fast habits and manners in a woman seem to him a fault in her taste; it is as if she wore fur slippers with her Court train. "Of course," he will say, apologetically, "this idea of mine is born of the absurd English conventionality which sleeps in all of us, nothing better; an Englishman is always conventional at heart let him live as he will."

He himself is the most unconventional of beings, appals his county, terrifies his relations, and irrevocably offends the bishop of his diocese; he has lived with Arabs, French artists, and wild men of the woods, and believes that he has not such a thing as a prejudice about him ; yet, at the bottom of his soul, there is this absurd feeling born of sheer conventionality—he cannot thoroughly like a light-minded woman. Absurd, indeed, in the times in which his lot is cast! He is quite ashamed of it.

Dorothy Usk does not favour the modern mode of having relays of guests for two days or three days; she thinks it makes a country house too like an hotel. She wishes her people to be perfectly well assorted, and then to stay with her at least a week, even two weeks or three weeks. People do not often object. Orme, Denton, and Surrenden are all popular places, and Surrenden is, perhaps, most popular of all.

"An ideal house," says Brandolin, who would not stay a day where he was not as free as air.

"It's too much like an hotel," grumbles the master of it, "and an hotel where the *table d'hôte* bell rings to deaf ears. Look how they all stray downstairs just as it pleases 'em! Lord! I remember in my poor mother's days, everybody had to be down to breakfast at nine o'clock every morning, as regularly as if they were charity children, and the whole lot of 'em were marched off to church on Sunday whether they liked it or not. The villagers used to line the path across the fields to see the great folk pass. Now, it's as much as ever Dolly can do to get a woman or two up in time to go with her. How things are changed, by Jove! And it isn't so very long ago, either."

"The march of intellect, my dear George," says Brandolin; "neither *le bon Dieu* or we are great folks any longer."

"Well, I think it's a pity," sighs Usk. "Everybody was happier then, and jollier too, though we do tear about so to try and get amused."

"There is still nothing to prevent you going to sleep in the big pew if it pleases you," replies Brandolin; "and Lawrence Hamilton always goes that he may look at Mrs. Curzon's profile as she sings; she is really saintly then. I think Sunday service is to Englishwomen what confession is to Catholic ladies; it sweeps all the blots off the week's tablets. It is convenient if illogical."

"You are very irreligious," says his host, who is invariably orthodox, when orthodoxy doesn't interfere with anything pleasant.

"Not more so than most people," says Brandolin. "I have even felt religious when I have been alone in the savannahs or in the jungle. I don't feel so in a wooden box covered with red velvet, with a curate bawling in my ears about the hewing in pieces of Agag."

"That's nothing to do with it," says Usk, "we're bound to set an example."

"That's why you doze in public, and Mrs. Curzon wears her big pearls, to lead the school children in the way they should go."

"That's nothing to do with it," repeats Lord Usk, somewhat crossly. He has a comfortable if indistinct idea that he does something patriotic, patriarchal, and highly praiseworthy in getting up an hour earlier than usual one Sunday out of three, and putting on a tall hat, a frock coat, and a pair of new gloves, to attend the village church for morning service when he is at Orme, Denton, or Surrenden in fine weather.

If he sleeps, what of that? There are curtains to the pew, and nobody sees him except the Babe, who takes fiendish rapture in catching big flies and releasing them from a careful little hand to alight on his father's forehead or nose. The Babe would define the Sunday morning as a horrid bore tempered by bluebottles.

" What a curiously conventional mind is the English mind," thinks Brandolin, when he is alone. " Carlyle is right, the gig is its standard. The gig is out of fashion as a vehicle, but the national mind remains the same as in the age of gigs ; content with the outside of things, clinging to the husk, to the shell, to the outward appearance, and satisfied with these. My dear friend puts on his chimney pot, then takes it off and snores in his pew, and thinks that he has done something holy which will sustain both Church and State, as he thinks that he prays when he buries his face in his hat and creases his trousers on a hassock. Mysterious consolations of the unfathomable human breast!"

CHAPTER V.

A few new people have come by the brake, and make their appearance at luncheon. More come by the five o'clock train, and are visible at six o'clock tea, which is always to be had in the library anytime before seven : dinner at all the Usk houses is always at nine. Brandolin's doctrines do not prevail with any of his acquaintances, although he, unlike most professors, emphasises them by example.

Amongst the people who come by the latter train are the great Mr. Wootton, very famous at London dinner parties, and Lady Gundrede Vansittart, whose dinners are the best in London.

"Where would those two people be if you brought the pulse and the rice you recommend into fashion?" says the host to Brandolin. "Take 'em away from the table they'd be good for nothing. He wouldn't say 'Bo' to a goose, and she wouldn't be be worth leaving a card upon. Believe me, my dear Guy, such *esprit* as there is left in us now-a-days is only brought out by eating."

"I think you invert all your reasonings," says Brandolin. "Say, rather, that too much eating has destroyed all *esprit*. Don't we eat all day long everywhere, or at least are expected to do so? You lament your ruined digestion. It is impossible to digest when time is only counted by what our beloved Yankees call square meals (why square I fail to fathom), and for women it is worse than for us, because they eat such quantities of sweet things we don't touch, and then the way they go in for caviare bread and butter, and anchovy sandwiches, and all kinds of rich cakes and *deux doigts de Madère,* or glasses of Kummel at the tea hour—it is frightful! I wonder they have any complexions at all left, even with the assistance of all the '*secrets de Vénus.*'"

"You won't alter 'em, my dear fellow," replied Usk, "if you put yourself out about it ever so much. If you were to marry a savage out of Formosa, or an Esquimaux, she'd take kindly to the caviare and the Kummel before a week was out, if you brought her to Europe. Why, look at dogs, you may keep 'em on biscuit and tripe if they live in the kennels, but if they once come to the dining-room they'll turn their noses up at a beefsteak if it isn't truffled!"

"Dogs, at least, stop short of the Kummel," says Brandolin, "but if you were to put together the sherry, the dry champagne, the liqueurs at tea, the brandy in the *chasse* at dinner, which a fashionable woman takes in the course of the day (not counting any pick-me-up that she may require in her own room), the amount would be something enormous—incredible! You would not believe the number of women who have cured me of an unhappy passion for them by letting me see what a lot they could drink."

"You will adore the Sabaroff, then. She never touches anything that I see, except tea."

"Admirable person! I am ready to adore her. Tell me more about her. By-the-way, who is she?"

"Oh, you must go to Dolly for biographies of her foreigners. I can't keep even their names in my head."

"Foreigners! What an expression!" cries Dorothy Usk, in disdain. "Since steam effaced frontiers, nobody but insular people like ourselves ever use such a term. Nationalities are obliterated."

She is very fond of Xenia Sabaroff; she has a great many warm attachments to women who help to make her house attractive.

" Nationalities are still discernible in different tobaccos," murmurs Brandolin. "The Havannah won't acknowledge an equal in the Cavour."

"Dolly don't know anything about her," continues Usk, clinging to the subject.

"Oh, my dear!" cried his wife, shocked, "when she is the niece of the great Chancellor and her mother was a Princess Dourtza."

"You don't know anything about her," repeats Usk, with that unpleasant obstinacy characteristic of men when they talk to their wives. "You met her in Vienna and took one of your crazes for her, and she may have sent a score of lovers to Siberia, or deserve to go there herself for anything you can tell.

foreigners."

" How absurd you are, and how *insular*," cries Dorothy Usk again. " ' Foreigners !' As if there were any foreigners in these days, when Europe is like one family !"

" A family which, like most families, squabbles and scratches pretty often then," says Usk, which seems to his wife a reply too vulgar to be worthy of contradiction. He is conscious that Xenia Sabaroff is a very great lady, and that her quarterings, backed by descent and alliance, are wholly irreproachable, indeed, written in that libro d'oro, the Almanac de Gotha, for all who chose to read.

Her descent and her diamonds are alike immaculate, but her character? He is too old-fashioned a Briton not to think it very probable that there is something *louche* there.

Usk is a Russophobist, as becomes a true Tory. He has a rooted impression that

all Russians are spies, when they are not
swindlers ; much as in the early years of
the century his grandsire had been positive
that all Frenchmen were assassins when
they were not dancing-masters. The White
Czar has replaced the Petit Caporal, and
the fur cap the cocked hat, in the eyes of
Englishmen of Usk's type, as an object of
dread and detestation. He would never be
in the least surprised if it turned out that
the real object of Madame Sabaroff's visit
to Surrenden were to have possible opportunities to examine the facilities of Wey-
mouth as a landing place for Kossacks out
of Muscovite corvettes.

" Russians are tremendous swells at
palaver," he says, with much contempt ;
" gammon you no end if you like to believe
'em ; but they've always some political
dodge or other behind it all."

" I don't say she isn't an agreeable
woman," he continues now : his admira-

tion of Madame Sabaroff is much mitigated by his sense that she has a rather derisive opinion of himself. " I don't say she isn't an agreeable woman, but she gives me the idea of artificiality—insincerity—mystery."

" Just because she's a Russian !" cries his wife, with disdain.

" My dear George," observes Brandolin, " there are preconceived ideas about all nationalities. As a rule, they are completely false. The received Continental idea is that an Englishman is a bluff, blunt, unpleasant, opinionated person; very cross, very clean too, it is true, but, on the strength of his tub and his constitution, despising all the rest of mankind. Now, how completely absurd such an opinion is. You yourself are an example of the *suaviter in modo, fortiter in re*, of which the true blue Briton always gives so admirable an example."

Usk laughs, but sulkily ; he has the

impression that his beloved friend is making fun of him, but he is not quite sure. He himself believes that he is an ideal Englishman; Brandolin is only half or a quarter of one; he does not shoot, wears furs in winter, only drinks very light Rhenish wine, never goes to any church, and never cuts his hair very short. Added to this, he has no fixed political opinion; except a general impression that England and the world in general are going down hill as fast as they can, "tobogganing," as they say in Canada, at the rate of fifty miles a minute, to land in the slough of Socialism, and be picked out of it by some military despot; democracy invariably ending in absolutism.

"What ridiculous rubbish about Russians," says his wife. "You might as well say that the *demoiselles-mannequins* at Worth's or Rodrigue's are conspiring for the Orleanists when they try on my clothes!"

" They are conspiring for the ruin of your family," says Usk, with a groan. "Whose purse can stand those Paris prices?"

"What an irrelevant remark!" cries Lady Usk. "You are always dragging money questions into everything."

" Those *faiseurs*, as you call 'em," continues Usk, unheeding, "are at the root of half the misery of society. Women get into debt up to their eyes for their toilettes, and they don't care what abominations they commit if they get enough out of it to go on plunging. Hundred-guinea gowns soon make up a pretty total when you change 'em three times a day."

" And if women are guys aren't the men furious?" asked his wife. "Even if they try to economise, aren't they always taunted with being dowdies? You none of you know anything about the cost of things, and you expect everybody to be *bien mise* on a halfpenny a day. When Boom saw me at Ascot this year he stared at me and whispered to me, 'Oh, I say, mother! you've got the same bonnet on you had at the Oaks. I do hope the other fellows won't notice it.' That is how he will speak to his wife some day, and yet I daresay, like you, he will expect her to get her bonnets from Virôt at ten francs a piece!"

Lady Usk is angry and roused.

" Look at my poor little sister," she goes on. "What a life that brute Mersey leads her about money. All those dreadfully plain girls to dress and nothing to do it on, and yet, if they are not all well got up, wherever they go to, he swears he is ashamed to be seen with them. You can't dress well, you can't do anything well, without spending money, and if you haven't money you must get into debt. That is as clear as that two and two are four.

Whenever do men remember their own extravagances? You smoke ten cigars a day; your cigars cost a shilling or eighteenpence each—that is, ten or fifteen shillings a day; five pounds a week, not counting your cigarettes! Good Heavens! Five pounds a week for sheer silly personal indulgence that your doctors tell you will canker your tongue and dry up your gastric juice! At all events, our toilettes don't hurt our digestion, and what would the world look like if women weren't well dressed in it? Your cigars benefit nobody, and only make your teeth yellow."

"Well, in a year they cost about what one ball gown does that's worn twice."

"I always wear mine three times, even in London," says Dorothy Usk, with conscious virtue. "But I don't see any sin in spending money. I think it ought to be spent. But you are always dragging money questions into everything, and Boom says that the Latin person, whom you and Lord Brandolin are always quoting, declares, most sensibly, that money should always be regarded as a means, never as an end, and if it is to be a means to anything must not it be spent before it can become so?"

"That's neither here nor there," replies her lord ; "and if Boom only reads his classics upside down like that he'd better leave 'em alone."

"You are never content. Most men would be delighted if a boy read *at all*."

"I don't know why, I'm sure," replies Usk, drearily. "Reading's going out, you know ; nobody'll read at all fifty years hence; poking about in guinea-pigs' stomachs, and giving long names to insects out of the coal-hole is what they call education now-a-

conjugal colloquy, and seeks to make a diversion on it, "that the boast of science is to send the Indian mails across seas and deserts in nine days. But that science cannot put in those mail bags a single letter equal to Voltaire's or the Sevigné's, and he doubts very much that there is one."

"It's an ill bird that fouls its own nest, or its own century," says Usk, grimly; "still, I'm very glad if those scientific prigs fall out amongst themselves."

"I think some people write charming letters still," says Dorothy Usk. "Of course when one is in a hurry—and one is almost always in a hurry——"

"Hurry is fatal, Lady Usk," says Brandolin. "It destroys style, grace, and harmony. It is the curse of our times. The most lovely thing in life is leisure, and we call it progress to have killed it."

"Read this letter," says his hostess, giving him one which she holds in her hand.

"There is nothing private in it, and nothing wonderful, but there is a grace in the expressions; whilst the English, for a foreigner, is absolutely marvellous."

" I thought there were no foreigners," says Usk; " I thought steam had effaced nationalities?"

His wife does not deign to reply.

Brandolin has taken the letter with hesitation. " Do you really think I may read it?"

" When I tell you to do so," says Dolly Usk, impatiently. "Besides, there is nothing in it, only it is pretty."

Brandolin reads; it is on very thick paper, almost imperceptibly scented, with a princess's crown embossed on it, and a gold X.

"It is very kind of you, dear Lady Usk, to have remembered a *solitaire* like myself in the midst of your charming children and your many joys. ('My many annoyances, she means,' interpolates Lady Usk.) I will be with you, as you so amiably wish, next Tuesday or Wednesday. I am for the moment in Paris, having been this month at Aix, not that I have any aches or pains myself, but a friend of mine, Marie Woronszoff, has many, and tries to cure them by warm sunshine and the cold douches which her physicians prescribe. There are many pleasant people here ; everyone is supposed to be very ill and suffering agony, but everyone laughs, flirts, plays, sits under the little tents under the trees, dances at the Casino, and eats a fair dinner as usual, so that if Pallida Mors be indeed amongst us, she looks just like everyone else. I came to Aix from my own place on the White Sea, and the gay groups, the bright alleys, the green embowered chálets, and the goatherds with their flocks which come tinkling their bells down the hillsides in all directions, all seem to me like an operetta of Offenbach's, spiritualised and washed with the pure daylight and the mountain air, but still Offenbach. How are your children? Do they still care for me? That is very sweet of them. A day at their years is as long as a season at mine. Assure them of my unforgetting gratitude. I shall be pleased to be in England again, and though I do not know Surrenden, my recollections of Orme tell me *d'avance* that I shall, in any house of yours, find the kindest of friends, the most sympathetic of companions. Say many things to your lord for me. I think he is only so discontented because the gods have been too good to him, and given him too completely everything he can desire. ('That's all *she* knows about it!' says Usk, *sotto voce*.) *Au revoir*, dear Lady Usk. Receive the assurance of my highest consideration, and believe in my sincere regard. *Bien à vous.*—XENIA P. SABAROFF."

"A very pretty letter," says Brandolin. "Many thanks," and he restores it to its owner.

"Bunkum!" says Usk.

"Not a bit in the world," says his wife, with contempt and indignation. "*She* does not 'pose' if you do!"

"My dear George," says Brandolin, "you are one of those thorough-going Britons who always think that everybody who doesn't deal in disagreeable remarks must be lying. Believe me, there are people who really 'see the side that's next the sun,'—even in a crab-apple."

"And deuced irritating, too, they are," says Usk, with emphasis. "'What a beastly bad day,' one says to 'em when it's pouring cats and dogs, and they answer: 'Oh, yes, but rain was so wanted, we must be thankful.' That's the kind of answer that would make a saint swear."

"You are not a saint and you swear

on small provocation," replies Brandolin. "To look at rain in that light argues true philosophy. Unfortunately, philosophy is too often strained to bursting in our climate, by having to contemplate rain destroying the crops. If we only had rain when we wanted it, I think the most unreasonable amongst us would view it with equanimity."

Rain is at that moment running down the painted panes of the Surrenden casements, and driving across the lawns and terraces of the Surrenden gardens. It makes Usk very cross: all the ensilage in the world will not console him for ripening corn beaten down in all directions, and young families of pheasants dying of cramp and pip in their ferny homes.

"Dig a big pit and cram your soaked grass into it; very well, I don't say no," he growls. "But what about your mildewed wheat? And where should we be if we had to undergo a blockade? I'm not against making more pasture, grazing's all very well ; but, if there's a war big enough to sweep the seas of the grain ships that come to us from the Colonies and the United States, where shall we be if we've nothing to eat but our own beef and mutton ? Beef and mutton are solid food, but I believe we should all go mad on them if we'd no bread to eat too."

" I'm all for pasture," replies Brandolin, " and, as the British Isles can never, under any cultivation whatever, feed all their population, we may as well dedicate ourselves to what is picturesque. I am fascinated by Laveleye's portrait of England when she shall have turned grazier exclusively ; it is lovely ; ' L'Angleterre redeviendra ce qu'elle était sous les Tudors, un grand parc vert, parsémé d'ormes et de chenês ou bœufs et moutons se promeneront dans des prairies sans limites.' "

" ' Prairies sans limites ?' How'll they

manage that when the land's to be all sliced up in little bits between peasant proprietors!" says Usk.

"I don't think Laveleye believes in peasant proprietors, though he *is* a professor of social economy."

"Social economy!" says Usk, with a groan. "Oh, I know that fool of a word! In plain English, it means ruin all round and fortune for a few d——d manufacturers."

"The d——d manufacturer is the principal outcome of two thousand centuries of Christianity, civilisation, and culture. The result is not perfectly satisfactory, or encouraging, one must admit," says Brandolin, as he reaches down a volume of eighteenth-century memoirs, and adds, with entire irrelevancy to manufacturers or memoirs: "Is she really as handsome as your children tell me?"

was here at Easter, and she turned their heads."

"Has she any lovers older than Babe?"

"She has left 'em in Russia if she has."

"A convenient distance to leave anything at; Italy and Russia are the only countries remaining to us, in which Messalina can still do her little murders comfortably without any fuss being made."

"She isn't Messalina, at least, I think not. But one never knows."

"No, one never knows till one tries," said Brandolin. And he wishes vaguely that the Russian woman were already here. He is fond of Surrenden and fond of all its people, but he is a little, a very little, bored. He sees that all Lady Usk's doves are paired, and he does not wish to disturb their harmony; possibly, because none of the feminine doves attract him. But he cannot flirt for ever with the children, because the children are not very often visible, and without flirting civilised life is dull, even for a man who is more easily consoled by ancient authors off the library shelves than most people can be.

This conversation occurs in the forenoon, in Lady Usk's boudoir. In the late afternoon, in the library, over their teacups, the ladies talk of Xenia Sabaroff. It is perceptible to Brandolin that they would prefer that she should not arrive.

"Is she so very good-looking?" he asks of Mrs. Wentworth Curzon.

"Oh, yes," replies that lady, with an accent of depreciation in her tones. "Yes, she is very handsome; but too pale, and her eyes too large. You know those Russian women are mere *paquets de nerfs*, shut up in their rooms all day and smoking so incessantly,—they have all that is worst in the Oriental and Parisienne mixed together."

"How very sad!" says Brandolin. "I don't think I have known one except

Princess Kraskawa : she went sleighing in all weathers, wore the frankest of gingerbread wigs, and was always surrounded by about fifty grandchildren."

Princess Kraskawa had been for many years ambassadress in London.

"Of course, there are exceptions," says Nina Curzon, "but generally, you know, they are very depraved, such inordinate gamblers, and so fond of morphine, and always *maladives.*"

" Ah," says Brandolin, pensively, " but the physical and moral perfection of Englishwomen always makes them take too high a standard : poor humanity toils hopelessly and utterly exhausted many miles behind them."

"Don't talk nonsense," says Mrs. Curzon, " we are no better than our neighbours, perhaps, but we are not afraid of the air ; we don't heat our houses to a thousand degrees above boiling point ; we don't gamble—at least not much—and we don't talk every language under the sun except our own, and yet not one of them grammatically."

"Decidedly," reflects Brandolin. "Lawrence must have looked too often at Madame Sabaroff. Sabaroff is dead, isn't he?" he asks aloud. "You know I have been out of society for a year; the whole map of Europe gets altered in one's absence."

"Sabaroff was shot in a duel four years ago," replies Mrs. Curzon; "a duel about her."

"What a fortunate woman! To get rid of a husband, and to get rid of him in such interesting circumstances! *C'est le comble de bonheur!*"

"That depends. With her it resulted in her exile from Court."

"Ah, to be sure, when Russians are naughty they are sent to live on their estates, as riotous children are dismissed to the nursery. Was she compromised, then?"

"Very much compromised; and both men were killed, for the adversary of Sabaroff had been wounded mortally, when, with an immense effort, he fired, and shot the Prince through the lungs."

"A pretty little melodrama. Who was the opponent?"

"Count Lustoff, a Colonel of the Guard. I wonder you did not hear of it, it made a stir at the time."

"I may have heard; when one doesn't know the people concerned, no massacre, even of the Innocents, makes any impression on one. And the result was that the lady had to leave the Imperial Court!"

"Yes; they do draw a line *there*."

Brandolin laughs; it tickles his fancy to hear Mrs. Wentworth Curzon condemning by implication the laxity of the Court of St. James.

"They can't send *us* to our estates," he replies, "the lands are so small and the railways are so close. Else it would have a very good effect if all our naughty people could be shut up inside their own gates, with nobody to speak to but the steward and the rector. Can you imagine anything that would more effectively contribute to correct manners and morals? But how very desolate London would look!"

"You think everybody would be exiled inside his own ring-fence?"

"*Her* own ring-fence—well, nearly everybody. There would certainly be no garden parties at Marlborough House."

Mrs. Wentworth Curzon is not pleased: she is a star of the first magnitude at Marlborough House.

"Why does she take this absent woman's character away?" thinks Brandolin, with a sense of irritation. "I will trust the Babe's instincts sooner than hers."

He does not know Xenia Sabaroff, but he admires the photograph of her which stands on the boudoir table, and he likes the tone of the letter written from Aix. With that spirit of contradiction which is inborn in human nature, he is inclined to disbelieve all that Nina Curzon has told him. Lustoff and Sabaroff probably both deserved their fates, and the departure from the Court of St. Petersburg might very possibly have been voluntary. He has a vague feeling of tenderness for the original of the photograph. It often happens to him to fall sentimentally and ephemerally in love with some unknown woman whose portrait he has seen, or of whose charms he has heard. Sometimes he has avoided knowing these in their actual life lest he should disturb his ideals. He is an imaginative man, with a great amount of leisure in which to indulge his fancies, and his knowledge of the world has not hardened

Surrey, in him.

"To think of all one knows about that hussy," he muses, as he smokes a cigar in his bedroom before dressing for dinner. By the uncomplimentary epithet he means Mrs. Wentworth Curzon. "Such a good fellow as Fred Curzon is too, a man who might have been made anything of, if she'd only treated him decently. When he married her he adored the ground she walked on, but before a week was out she began to fret him, and jeer at him, and break him in, as she called it; he was too poor for her, and too slow for her, and too good for her, and she was vilely cruel to him—it's only women who can be cruel like that; she's had more lovers than anybody living, and she's taken every one of 'em for money; nothing but money. Old Melton gave her the Park-lane House, and

Glamorgan gave her her emeralds, and Dartmoor paid her Paris bills for ten years, and Riverston takes all her stable expenses. Everything she does is done for money, and if she puts any heart at all now into this thing with Lawrence, it is only because she's getting older and so getting jealous—they always do as they get on —and then she calls Russians dissolute and depraved. Good Lord!"

With which he casts aside his cigar, and resigns himself to his servant's hands as the second gong sounds.

CHAPTER VI.

The very bachelor rooms at Surrenden are
conducive to reverie and indolence, cosily
comfortable and full of little attentions for
the guest's *bien être*, amongst which there
is a printed paper which is always laid on
the dressing-table in every room at this
house; it contains the latest telegrams of
public news which come every afternoon
from a London news agency.

"I daresay to the political fellows they
are delightful," reflects Brandolin, as he
glances down the lines, "but to me they
unpleasantly re-call an uncomfortable world.
I don't dine the worse, certainly, for knowing that there is a revolution in Patagonia,
or an earthquake in Bolivar, but neither

do I dine the better for being told that the French Government is *destituant* all moderate Prefets in favour of immoderate ones. It is very interesting, no doubt, but it doesn't interest me, and I think the possession of these fresh scraps of prosaic news spoils dinner conversation."

Brandolin does not consider it conversation to say "Have you seen so and so?" or, "What a sad thing such and such is, isn't it?" He likes persiflage, he likes banter, he likes argument, he likes antithesis, he likes brilliancy, and the dinner tables of the epoch seldom offer these good things with their Metternich hock and Mouton Rothschild. He is fond of talking himself, and he can be also a very good listener. If you cannot give the *quid quo pro* in hearing, as in speaking, you may be immensely clever, but you will be immediately pronounced a bore, like Macaulay and Madame de Stael. Brandolin likes talking, not for the sake of showing himself off, but for the sake of being amused, of eliciting the opinions and observing the minds of others, and he is convinced that if the conversational art were cultured as it used to be in the Paris of the Bourbons, life would become more refined, more agreeable, more sympathetic, and less given over to gross pleasures of the appetites.

"Children should be taught to talk," he observed one day to Lady Usk, "and they should not be allowed to be slovenly in their speech any more than in their dress. You would not let them enter your presence with unbrushed hair, but you do let them use any bald, slangy, or inappropriate words which come uppermost to them. There is so much in the choice of words! A beautiful voice is a delicious thing, but it avails little without the usage of apt and graceful phrases. Did you ever

her."

"We are always in such a hurry," says
Lady Usk, which is her habitual explanation of anything in which her generation
is at fault. "And hurry is always vulgar,
you know, as you said the other day; it
cannot help itself."

"You are a purist, my dear Brandolin,"
says Lady Dolgelly, who hates him.

" 'Purity, daughter of sweet virtues mild!' "
murmurs Brandolin. "Alas! my dear
ladies, I cannot hope that she dwells with
me in any form! When she has a home
in your own gentle breasts, who can hope
that she would ever take shelter in a
man's?"

a little more cordially than before. There is not a very good feeling towards him amongst any of the ladies at Surrenden; he does not make love to them, he does not endeavour to alter existing arrangements in his favour; it is generally felt that he would not care to do so. What can you expect from a man who sits half his days in a library?

The Surrenden library is well stored, an elegant and lettered lord of the eighteenth century having been a bibliophile. It is a charming room, panelled with inlaid woods, and with a ceiling painted after Tiepolo; the bookcases are built into the wall, so that the books seem *chez eux*, and are not mere lodgers or visitors; oriel windows look on to a portion of the garden laid out by Beaumont. One window has been cut down to the ground, an anachronism and innovation, indeed, somewhat impairing the uniformity of the room. The present

Lady Usk had it done, but one forgives her the sacrilege when one feels how pleasant it is to walk out from the mellow shadows of the library on to the smooth-shaven grass, and gather a rose with one hand whilst holding an eighteenth-century author with the other.

It is in the smaller library adjacent, filled with modern volumes, that five o'clock tea is always to be had, with all the abundant demoralising abominations of caviare, Kummel, etc. It is a gay room, with *dessus des portes* after Watteau, and every variety of couch and of lounging chair. "Reading made easy" somebody calls it. But there is little reading done either in it or in the big library: Brandolin, when he goes there, finds himself usually alone, and can commune as he chooses with Latin philosophy and Gaulois wit.

"You *used* to read, George?" he says to his host in expostulation.

"Yes, I used—ages ago," says Usk, with a yawn.

Brandolin looks at him with curiosity.

"I can understand a man who has never read," he replies, "but I cannot understand a man losing the taste for reading if he has ever had it. One can dwell contented in Bœotia if one have never been out of it, but to go back to Bœotia after living in Attica——"

"It's one's life does it."

"What life? One has the life one wishes."

"That's the sort of thing a man says who hasn't married."

"My dear George! you cannot pretend that your wife would prevent your reading Latin and Greek, or even Sanscrit! I am sure she would much sooner you read them than — well— than did other things you do do."

"I don't say she would prevent me,"

you ?"

"There's no time for anything," says Usk, gloomily. "There's such heaps of things to see to, and such numbers of places to go to, and then one lives *au jour le jour*, and one gets into the swim and goes on, and then there's the shooting, and when there isn't the shooting there's the season and the racing."

"I lead my own life," Brandolin remarks.

"Yes; but you don't mind being called eccentric."

"No; I don't mind it in the least. If they say nothing worse of me I am grateful."

Brandolin smiles.

A sixth part of most days his host passes leaning back in some easy chair with a cigar in his mouth, whether his venue be Surrenden, Orme, Denton, the smoking-room of a club, or the house of a friend; whether London or the country. Usk's own view of himself is of a man entirely devoted to, and sacrificed to business, politics, the management of his estates, and the million and one affairs which perpetually assail him; but this is not the view which his friends take of him.

Whenever is the view that our friends take of us our view?

"Once a scholar always a scholar, it seems to me," says Brandolin. "I could

as soon live without air as without books,"
and he quotes Cowley—

"Books should, like business, entertain the day,"

"You don't continue the quotation," says
Usk, with a smile.

"*Autres temps, autres mœurs*," says Brandolin. He laughs and gets up; it is four
in the afternoon; the delicious green garden
is lying bathed in warm amber light; one
of the peacocks is turning round slowly
with all his train displayed; he seems never
to tire of turning round.

"How exactly that bird is like some
politicians one could name," says Brandolin.
"Do you know that this charming garden
always reminds me of St. Hubert's Lea;
our west garden, I mean? I think the
same man must have laid them out. Is it
not Bulwer-Lytton who says that so long
as one has a garden, one always has one
room which is roofed by Heaven?"

"A Heaven mitigated by gardeners'

wages—very considerably mitigated," says Usk.

"You are cynical, George, and your mind is running on pounds, shillings, and pence—an offence against nature on such a day as this. There is nothing so demoralising as to think of money."

"To have debts and not to think of 'em is more so ; and Boom——"

"Sell something of his that he likes very much, to pay his debts ; that's the only way I know of to check a boy at the onset. Your father did it with me the very first time I owed twenty pounds, and he read me a lesson I never forgot. I have been eternally obliged to him ever since."

"What did he sell?"

"My cob, a cob I adored. I wept like a child, but he didn't see my tears. What I saved up next month to trace out that cob and buy him back at twice his value ;— what I denied myself to make up the money—nobody would believe ; and the beast wasn't easy to find ; some dealer had taken him over to Ireland."

"That could be done with you," says Usk, gloomily. "It would be no use to do it with Boom, his mother would buy him some other horse the next day. You've no chance to bring up a boy decently if he's got a mother!"

"The reverse is the received opinion of mankind," said Brandolin, "but I believe there's something to be said for your view. No end of women have no idea of bringing up their children, and when they ought to be ordered a flogging they fondle them."

"Dolly does," says her husband. "What's a woman's notion of a horse ? That he must have slender legs, a coat like satin, and be fed on apples and sugar ; still, they saw his mouth till he half-dislocates his neck, and tear his ribs open with their spur. They're just as unreasonable with their children."

"Who is *that* woman?" says Brandolin, making a step across the window and into the garden. "Now, I am perfectly certain that is Madame Sabaroff, without your saying so."

"Then I needn't say so," replies Usk. "I wonder when she came. They didn't expect her till to-morrow."

They both look at a lady in one of the distant alleys walking between the high, green walls. She is dressed in some soft cream-coloured stuff, with quantities of lace. She carries a sunshade of the same hue. She has a tall cane in her other hand. On either side of her are the Ladies Alexandra and Hermione, and before her gambols in his white sailor clothes, with his blue silk stockings and his silver-buckled shoes, the Babe.

"Decidedly the Sabaroff," says Usk. "Won't you come and speak to her?"

"With pleasure," says Brandolin. "Even if the Babe brains me with the cane!"

He looks very well as he walks bareheaded over the grass and along the green alley. He wears a loose brown velvet coat, admirably made, and brown breeches and stockings; his legs are as well made as his coat; the sun shines on his curling hair, there is a degagé, picturesque, debonnair, yet distinguished, look about him which pleases the eyes of Xenia Sabaroff as they watch him draw near.

"Who is that person with your father?" she asks. The children tell her, all speaking at once.

She recognises the name; she has heard of him often in the world, and has read those books which praise solitude and a dinner of herbs. "I doubt his having been alone very long, however," she reflects, as she looks at him. A certain unlikeness in him to Englishmen in general, some women who are fond of him fancifully trace to the fact that the first Brandolin was a Venetian, who fled for his life from the Republic, and made himself conspicuous and acceptable for his talents alike as a lutist and a swordsman at the Court of Henry the Second. "It can't count, it's so very far away," he himself objects ; but perhaps it does count. Of all things in-effaceable, the marks of race are the most indelible.

The Venetian Brandolin married the daughter of a Norman knight, and his descendants became affectionate sons of England, and held their lands of St. Hubert's Lea safely under the Wars of the Roses, of the Commonwealth, and of the Jacobites. They were always noticeable for scholarly habits and artistic tastes, and in the time of George II., the Lord Brandolin of the period did much to enrich his family mansion and diminish the family fortunes, by his importations of Italian artists. The house at St. Hubert's Lea is very beautiful, but it requires much more to keep it up than the present owner possesses. He is often urged to let it, but he scouts the idea. "You might as well ask me to sell the Brandolin portraits, like Charles Surface," he says, angrily, whenever his more intimate friends venture on the suggestion. So the old house stands in its warm-hued and casket-like loveliness, empty, save for his occasional visits, and the presence of many old and devoted servants.

"An interesting woman," he thinks now, as he exchanges with the Princess Sabaroff the usual compliments and commonplaces of a presentation. "Russians are always interesting: they are the only women about whom you feel that you know very little; they are the only women who, in this chatterbox of a generation, *tout en dehors* as it is, preserve some of the vague charm of mystery—and what a charm that is!"

His reasons for admiring her are not those of the Babe and his sisters, but he admires her almost as much as they. Brandolin, who, in his remote travels, has seen a great deal of that simple nature which is so much lauded by many people, has a great appreciation of well-dressed women, and Madame Sabaroff is admirably dressed, from her long loose cream-coloured gloves to her bronze shoes with their miniature diamond clasps.

"Didn't I tell you?" whispers the Babe, climbing up behind Brandolin.

"Yes, you did," returned Brandolin, "and you were quite right; but it is abominably bad manners to whisper, my dear Cecil."

The Babe subsides into silence with hot cheeks; when anybody calls him Cecil he is conscious that he has committed some flagrant offence.

"Those brats are always bothering you, Princess," says their father.

"They are very kind to me," replies Xenia Sabaroff, in English which has absolutely no foreign accent. "They make me feel at home! What a charming place this is! I like it better than your castle, what is its name, where I had the pleasure to visit you at Easter?"

"Orme," replies its master. "Oh, that's beastly — a regular barn — obliged to go there just for show, you know."

"Orme was built by Inigo Jones, and the ingratitude to fortune of its owner is a constant temptation to providence to deal in thunderbolts, or have matches left about by housemaids," says Brandolin.

"I think Lord Usk has not a contented mind," says Madame Sabaroff, amused.

"Contented! By Jove, who should be, when England's going to the dogs as fast as she can?"

"'Our constitution is established on a
nice equipoise, with dark precipices and
deep waters all around it.' So said Burke,"
replies Brandolin. "At the present moment
everybody has forgotten the delicacy of this
nice equipoise, and one day or other it will
lose its balance and topple over into the
deep waters and be engulphed. Myself,
I confess, I do not think that time is very
far distant."

"I hope it is: I am very much attached
to England," replies the Princess Xenia,
gravely, "and to naughty English boys,"
she adds, passing her hand over the shining
locks of the Babe.

"She must be in love with an Englishman," thinks Brandolin, with the one-sided

construction which a man is always ready to place on the words of a woman. "Must we go indoors?" he asks, regretfully, as she is moving towards the house. "It is so pleasant in these quaint, green arbours. To be under a roof on such a summer afternoon as this, is to fly in the face of a merciful Creator with greater ingratitude than Usk's ingratitude to Inigo Jones."

"But I have scarcely seen my hostess," says Madame Sabaroff; nevertheless, she resigns herself to a seat in a yew tree cut like a helmet.

There are all manner of delightful old-fashioned flowers, such flowers as Disraeli gave to the garden of Corisande, growing near in groups encircled by clipped box-edging.

Those disciples of Pallas Athene who render the happy lives of the Surrenden children occasionally a burden to them, seize at that moment on their prey and bear them off to the schoolroom; the Babe goes to his doom sullenly: he would be tearful, only that were too unmanly.

"Why do you let those innocents be tortured, George?" asks Brandolin.

"'Books should, like business, entertain the day,'" replies Usk; "so you said, at least, just now. Their governesses are of the same opinion."

"That is not the way to make them love books, to shut them up against their wills on a summer afternoon."

"How will you educate your children when you have 'em, then?"

"He always gets out of any impersonal argument by putting some personal question," complains Brandolin to Madame Sabaroff. "It is a common device, but always an unworthy one. Because a system is very bad, it does not follow that I alone, of all men, must be prepared with a better one. I think if I had children, I would not have them taught in that way at all. I should get the wisest old man I could find, a Samuel Johnson touched with a John Ruskin, and should tell him to make learning delightful to them, and associated, as far as our detestable climate would allow, with open-air studies in cowslip meadows and under hawthorn hedges. If I had only read dear Horace at school, should I ever have loved him as I do? No, my old tutor taught me to feel all the delight and the sweet savour of him, roaming in the oak woods of my own old place."

"I am devoutly thankful," says his host, "that Dorothy, amongst her many caprices, had never had the fancy you have for a Dr. Johnson *doublé* with a John Ruskin, to correct my quotations, abuse my architecture, and make prigs of the children."

"Prigs!" exclaimed Brandolin. "Prigs! When did ever real scholarship and love of nature make anything approaching to a prig? Science and class-rooms make prigs, not Latin verse and cowslip meadows."

"That is true, I think," says the Princess Xenia, with her serious smile.

"If they are beginning to agree with one another, I shall be *de trop*," thinks Usk, who is very good-natured to his guests, and popular enough with women not to be resigned to play what is vulgarly termed "second fiddle" (though why an expression borrowed from the orchestra should be vulgar it were hard to say). So he goes a few paces off to speak to a gardener; and by degrees edges away towards the house, leaving Brandolin and Madame Sabaroff to themselves in the green yew helmet arbour.

Brandolin is in love with his subject and does not abandon it.

"It is absurd," he continues, "the way in which children are made to loathe all scholarship by its association with their own pains and subjection. A child is made, as a punishment, to learn by rote fifty lines of Virgil. Good Heavens! It ought rather to be as a reward that he should be allowed to open Virgil! To walk in all those delicious paths of thought should be the highest pleasure that he could be brought to know. To listen to the music of the poets should be at once his privilege and his recompense. To be deprived of books should be. on the contrary, his cruellest chastisement!"

"He would be a very exceptional child, surely, if he thought so?" says Madame Sabaroff.

"I was not an exceptional child," he answers, "but that is how I was brought up and how I felt."

"You had an exceptional training, then?"

"It ought not to be exceptional: that is just the mischief. Up to the time I was seventeen. I was brought up at my own place (by my father's directions in his will) by a most true and reverent scholar, whom I loved as Burke loved Shackleton. He died, God rest his soul! but the good he left behind him lives after him ; whatever grains of sense I have shown, and whatever follies I have avoided, both what I am and what I am not, are due to him, and it is to him that I owe the love of study which has been the greatest consolation and the purest pleasure of my life. That is why I pity so profoundly these poor Rochfort children, and the tens of thousands like them, who are being educated by the commonplace, flavourless, cramming system which people call education. It may be education ; it is not culture. What will the Babe always associate with his Latin themes ? Four walls, hated books, inky, aching fingers and a headache. Whereas, I never see a Latin

line in a newspaper, be it one ever so
hackneyed, without pleasure, as at the face
of an old friend, and whenever I repeat to
myself the words of one, I always smell
the cowslips, and the lilac, and the hawthorn of the spring mornings when I was
a boy."

Xenia Sabaroff looked at him with some
little wonder and more approval.

"My dear lord," she says, seriously, "I
think in your enthusiasm you forget one
thing, that there is ground on which good
seed falls and brings forth flowers and fruit,
and there is other ground on which the
same seed, be it strewn ever so thickly,
lies always barren. Without under-rating
the influences of your tutor, I must believe
that had you been educated at an English
public school, or even in a French Lycée,
you would still have become a scholar, still
have loved your books."

"Alas, Madame!" says Brandolin, with

a little sigh. "Perhaps I have only been what Matthew Arnold calls 'a foiled circuitous wanderer' in the orbit of life!"

"I imagine that you have not very often been foiled," replies the lady, with a smile, "and wandering has a great deal to be said in its favour, especially for a man. Women are happiest, perhaps, at anchor."

"Women used to be: not our women; *nous avons changé tout cela.* But I have bored you too much with myself and my opinions."

"No, you interest me," says his companion, with a serious serenity which deprives the words of all sound of flattery or encouragement. "I have long admired your writings," she adds, and Brandolin colours a little with gratification. The same kind of phrase is said to him on an average five hundred times a year, and his usual emotion is either ennui or irritation. The admiration of fools is folly

and humiliates him. But the admiration
of as lovely a woman as Xenia Sabaroff
would lay a flattering unction to the soul
of any man, even if she were absolutely
mindless ; and she gives him the impression that she has a good deal of mind,
and one out of the common order.

"My writings have no other merit," he
says, after the expression of his sense of
the honour she does him, "than being absolutely the chronicle of what I have seen
and what I have thought ; and I think
they are expressed in tolerably pure English,
though that is claiming a great deal in
these times ; for since John Newman laid
down the pen there is scarcely a living
Briton who can write his own tongue with
eloquence and purity."

"I think it must be very nice to leave
off wandering if one has a home," replies
Madame Sabaroff, with a slight sigh, which
gave him the impression, that though, no

doubt, she had many houses, she had no home. "Where is your place that you spoke of just now, the place where you learned to love Horace?"

Brandolin is always pleased to speak of St. Hubert's Lea. He has a great love for it, and for the traditions of his race, which make many people accuse him of great family pride, though, as has been well said *apropos* of a greater man than Brandolin, it is rather that sentiment which the Romans defined as piety. When he talks of his old home he grows eloquent, unreserved, cordial ; and he describes, with an artist's touch, its antiquities, its land-scapes, and its old - world and sylvan charms.

"It must be charming to care for any place so much as that," says his companion, after hearing him with interest.

"I think one cares more for places than for people," he replies.

At that moment there is a little bustle under a very big cedar near at hand ; servants are bringing out folding tables, folding chairs, a silver camp kettle, cakes, fruit, cream, liqueurs, sandwiches, wines, all those items of an afternoon tea on which Brandolin has animadverted with so much disgust in the library an hour before. Lady Usk has chosen to take these murderous compounds out of doors in the west garden. She herself comes out of the house with a train of her guests around her.

"Adieu to rational conversation," says Brandolin, as he rises with regret from his seat under the evergreen helmet.

Xenia Sabaroff is pleased at the expres-

sion. She is too handsome for men often
to speak to her rationally; they usually
plunge headlong into attempts at homage
and flattery, of which she is nauseated.

CHAPTER VII.

"How do you like Lord Brandolin?" says Lady Usk, when she can say so unobserved.

"I like him very much," replies Madame Sabaroff. "He is what one would expect him to be from his books: and that is so agreeable—and so rare."

Dorothy Usk is not pleased. She does not want her Russian Phœnix to admire Brandolin. She has arranged an alliance in her own mind between the Princess Sabaroff and her own cousin, Alan, Lord Gervase, whom she is daily expecting at Surrenden. Gervase is a man of some note in diplomacy and society; she is proud of him, she is attached to him, she desires to see him ultimately fill all offices of State that the ambition of an Englishman can aspire to; and Xenia Sabaroff is so enormously rich, as well as so unusually handsome, that it would be a perfectly ideal union; and, desiring it infinitely, the mistress of Surrenden, with that tact which distinguishes herself, has never named Lord Gervase to the Princess Sabaroff nor the Princess Sabaroff to Lord Gervase. He is to be at Surrenden in a week's time. Now, she vaguely wishes that Brandolin had not these eight days' start of him. But, then, Brandolin, she knows, will only flirt; that is to say, if the Russian lady allows him to do so; he is an unconscionable flirt, and never means anything by his tenderest speeches. Brandolin, she knows, is not a person who will ever marry; he has lost scores of the most admirable opportunities, and rejected the fairest and best filled hands that have been offered to him.

To the orderly mind of Lady Usk, he represents an Ishmael for ever wandering in wild woods, outside the pale of general civilisation. She can never see why people make such a fuss with him. She does not say so, because it is the fashion to make the fuss, and she never goes against fashion. A very moral woman herself, she is only as charitable and elastic as she is to naughty people because such charity and elasticity is the mark of good society in the present day. Without it, she would be neither popular nor well-bred, and she would sooner die than fail in being either.

"Why don't you ever marry, Lord Brandolin?" asks Dorothy Usk the next day. "Why have you never married?"

"Because he's much too sensible," growls her husband, but adds, with infinite compassion: "He'll have to, some day, or the name will die out."

your very grammatical expression," assents Brandolin. " I don't wish the name to die out, and there's nobody to come after me except the Southesk-Vanes, who detest me as I detest them."

" Well, then, why not make some marriage, at once?" says Lady Usk. " I know so many charming——"

Brandolin arrests the sentence with a deprecatory gesture. " Dear Lady Usk, *please !* I like you so much, I wouldn't for worlds have you mixed up in anything which would probably, or, at least, very possibly, make me so much dislike you in the years to come."

Usk gives a laugh of much enjoyment.

His wife is slightly annoyed. She does not like this sort of jesting.

" You said a moment ago that you must marry !" she observes, with some impatience.

" Oh, there is no positive ' must ' about it," says Brandolin, dubiously. " The name doesn't matter greatly, after all; it is only that I don't like the place to go to the Southesk - Vanes; they are my cousins, Heaven knows how many times removed; they have most horrible politics, and they are such dreadfully prosaic people that I am sure they will destroy my gardens, poison my Indian beasts, strangle my African birds, turn my old servants adrift, and make the country round hideous with high farming."

"Marry, then, and put an end to any possibility so dreadful," says Dorothy Usk.

Brandolin gets up and walks about the room. It is a dilemma which has often been present to his mind in various epochs of his existence.

"You see, my dear people," he says, with affectionate confidence, "the real truth of the matter is this. A good woman is an admirable creation of Providence, for certain uses in her generation; but she is tiresome. A naughty woman is delightful; but then she is, if you marry her, compromising. Which am I to take of the two? I should be bored to death by what Renan calls *la femme pure,* and against *la femme tarée* as a wife, I have a prejudice. The women who would amuse me, I would not marry if I could, and as, if I were bored, I should leave my wife entirely and go to the Equator or the Pole, it would not be honest in me to sacrifice a virgin to the mere demands of my family pride."

Lady Usk feels shocked, but she does not like to show it, because it is so old-fashioned and prudish and *arrieré* now-a-days to be shocked at anything.

"I have thought about it very often, I assure you," continues Brandolin, "and sometimes I have really thought that I would marry a high-caste Hindoo woman. They are very beautiful, and their forms far more exquisite than any European's, wholly uncramped as they are by any stays, and accustomed to spend so many hours on all kinds of arts for the embellishment of the skin."

"I don't think, you know," Lady Usk interposes hastily, to repress more reminiscences, "that you need be afraid of the young girls of our time being innocent; they are *éveillées* enough, Heaven knows, and experienced enough in all conscience."

"Oh, but that is odious," says Brandolin, with disgust. "The girls of the day are horrible; nothing is unknown to them; they smoke, they gamble, they flirt without decency or grace, their one idea is to marry for sake of a position which will let them go as wild as they choose, and for the sake of heaps of money which will sustain their unconscionable extravagance. Lord deliver me from any one of them! I would sooner see St. Hubert's Lea cut up into allotment - grounds than save it from the

Southesk-Vanes by marrying a *débutante* with her mind fixed on establishing herself, and her youthful memories already full of dead-and-gone flirtations. No! let me wait for Dodo, if you will give me permission to educate her."

"Dodo will never be educated out of flirting; she is born for it." says her father, "and she will be a handful when she gets into society. I'm afraid you would return her to us, and sigh for your high-caste Hindoo."

"Pray, how would you educate her; what is missing in her present education?" asks Lady Usk, somewhat piqued at what he implies.

"I would let her see a great deal more of her mother than she is allowed to do," says Brandolin; "where could she take a better model?" he adds, with a bow of much grace.

Her mother is not sure whether she

ought to be flattered or offended. Brandolin has a way of mingling graceful compliments and implied censure with so much skill and intricacy, that to disentangle them is difficult for those whom he would at once flatter and rebuff. "One never quite knows what he means," she thinks, irritably. "I do believe he intends to imply that I neglect my children !"

Brandolin seems to her an unpleasant man ; eccentric, discourteous, and immoral. She cannot imagine what George or the world sees to admire and like so much in him.

"Lord Brandolin actually declares that black women have much better figures than we have," she says, an hour later to Leila Faversham.

"Black women !" exclaims that lady, in unspeakable horror.

"Well, Hindoos ; it is the same thing," says Lady Usk, with that ignorance of her

Indian fellow-subjects which is characteristic of English society, from the highest strata to the lowest.

"Oh, he is always so odd, you know," says Mrs. Faversham, as of a person whom it is hopeless even to discuss. Brandolin is indeed so odd that he has never perceived her own attractions. What can seem odder to a pretty woman than that?

Leila Faversham tells Lady Dawlish ten minutes later that Brandolin has confessed that he only likes black women. "Isn't it horrid? He actually has numbers of them down in Warwickshire, just as he keeps the Indian animals and the African birds."

"How very shocking!" says Lady Dawlish. "But I daresay it is very economical; they only eat a spoonful of rice and wear a yard of calico, you know, and as he is so poor that must suit him."

Lady Dawlish tells this fact to Nina Curzon, adding various embellishments of her fancy ; Mrs. Curzon thinks the notion new and amusing ; she writes of it that morning to a journal of society which she occasionally honours with news of her world, not from want of the editor's fees, but from the amusement it affords her to destroy the characters of her acquaintances. The journal will immediately, she knows, produce a mysterious but sensational paragraph regarding the black women in Warwickshire, or some other article headed "An Hereditary Legislator at Home." Brandolin is a person whom it is perfectly safe to libel : he is very indolent, very contemptuous, and he never by any chance reads a newspaper.

"An extremely interesting woman," muses Brandolin that evening, as he dresses for dinner. "Interesting, and, moreover, with something original, something mysterious and suggestive in her. Despite Lady Usk, there is a difference still in different nationalities. I could still swear to an English-woman anywhere, if I only saw the back of her head and her shoulders. No English-woman could have the delicious languor of Madame Sabaroff's movements."

She interests him; he decides to stay on at Surrenden.

When he sees her at dinner he is still more favourably impressed.

Her figure is superb, and her sleeveless gown shows the beauty of her bust and arms; she has a flat band of diamonds, worn between the elbow and the shoulder of the right arm. The effect is singular, but good.

"It is to show that she has the muscle developed between the shoulder and the elbow," says old Sir Adolphus, who is learned in sculpture and anatomy. "You know, not one woman in ten thousand has it; and for want of it their arms fall in above the elbow. I have heard sculptors say so a hundred times. She has it, and so she wears that flat bracelet to emphasise the fact."

Brandolin feels annoyed. There is no reason in life why he should object to Madame Sabaroff having any number of affectations and vanities, or why he should mind hearing this handsome old *viveur* discuss them; but he is annoyed by both facts.

There is not a plain woman amongst the guests at Surrenden, some are even far beyond the average of good looks, and all have that *chic* which lends in itself a kind of beauty to the woman of the world. But the handsomest of them all, Nina Curzon herself, pales beside the beautiful pallor of the Russian lady, contrasted as it is with the splendour of her jewels, the red rose of her lips, and the darkness of her eye-lashes and eyes.

At dinner, Xenia Sabaroff does not speak

fatigued one.

Brandolin is opposite to her: as there are no ornaments or flowers on the table higher than eight inches, he can contemplate her at his leisure across the field of shed rose leaves which is between them. Finding that she is so silent, he talks in his best fashion, in his most reckless, antithetical, picturesque manner; he perceives he gains her attention, though he never directly addresses her.

He also makes Mr. Wootton furious. Mr. Wootton has half-a-dozen good stories untold; his method of getting good stories is ingenious; he procures obscure but clever memoirs, French and English, which are wholly forgotten, alters their most piquant anecdotes a little, and fits them on to living and famous personages; the result is admirable, and has earned him his great reputation as a *raconteur* of contemporary

" Brandolin is *so* amusing when he likes," says Lady Arthur Audley, incautiously, to this suppressed and sullen victim.

" A monologuist, a monologuist!" replies Mr. Wootton, with a deprecatory accent.

Lady Arthur is silenced, for she has not the slightest idea what a monologuist is. She fancies it means some kind of a sect like the Mormons, and Brandolin is so odd that he may possibly belong to a sect, or may have founded one, like Lawrence Oliphant. She remembers the black women that they talked of, and does not like to ask, being a sensitive person, very delicate-minded and perfectly proper, except her one little affair with Sir Hugo, which everybody says is most creditable to her, Arthur Audley being the scamp that he is.

Dinner over, Brandolin finds a pleasant seat on a low chair behind the bigger chair on which Madame Sabaroff is reclining; other men devoted to other women look longingly at her; some approach; Brandolin comprehends why she is not beloved in her generation by her own sex.

After a time she is induced to sing; she has a very sweet voice of great power, with much pathos in it: she sings Volkslieder of her own country, strange, yearning, wistful songs, full of the vague mystical melancholy of the Russian peasant. She ceases to sing abruptly, and walks back to seat; her diamonds gleam in the light like so many eyes of fire. Brandolin has listened in silence, conscious of a troubled pleasure within himself, which is invariably the herald of one of those attachments which have so often at once embellished and disturbed his existence.

Like all romantic people, his heart is much younger than his years. It has not been scarred by any one of those tragic passions which, like fire on a hillside, wither up all green things, so that not a blade of grass will grow where it has passed. He has usually found love only the most agreeable of pastimes. He has always wondered why anybody allows it to tear their life to tatters, as a bad actor tears a fine piece of blank verse.

An uncle of his possessed an Aphrodite in Paphian marble which had been dug up in a vineyard at Luna, and a work of great beauty of the second period of Greek art. A lover of pleasure, but withal a philosopher, his uncle treasured and adored this statue, and whenever he felt that any living woman was getting more power over him than he liked, he compared her in his mind with the Luna Venus, and found that the human creature's defects outbalanced her charms, and thus reduced the potency of the latter to more reasonable dimensions.

Instead of his uncle's Luna goddess, Brandolin keeps in some remote and sealed-up nook of his mind a certain ideal ; now and then he remembers it, takes it out and looks at it, and it has usually served with him at such moments the purpose which the Luna marble served with his uncle.

As he saunters towards the smoking-room with his hands in the pockets of a loose velvet jacket, he summons this useful resident of his brain, intending to banish with it the remembrance, the too enervating remembrance, of Xenia Sabaroff. But to his surprise they seem very like one another, and their features blend confusedly into one.

" And I know nothing at all about this lady, except that she has a voice like Albani's, big jewels, and a Russian name !" he thinks, with some derision of himself :

the smokers do not find him amusing, while his companions seem to him insufferably tiresome. He hears the echo of Madame Sabaroff's grave, low, melodious voice, and is not in temper for the somewhat *scabreux* jests of the smoking-room. He thinks that it is all very well for boys to like that sort of salacious talk, but it seems to him intolerably absurd that men of his own age, and older, should find any kind of savour in it.

They tease him about the black women, moreover, and for once he is not easy enough to be good-tempered and indifferent. He answers contemptuously and irritably, and, of course, all his friends suppose, which they had not supposed before, that there is, after all, some truth in Mrs. Curzon's anecdote.

"What stupid stories that old *blagueur* Wootton has told, and what beastly ones Fred Ormond has related; and all as if they were something new, too: as if the one weren't taken out of the manuscripts at Bute House, and the other out of last week's *Figaro!* If men won't be original, or can't be, why don't they hold their tongues? And what fools we are to sit shut up with gaslights and tobacco on such a night as this; a night for Lorenzo and Jessica, for Romeo and Juliet!" he thinks, as he stands awhile at the open window of his own bedroom.

It is three o'clock, there is a faint, suggestive light which means the dawn, young birds are twittering, there is a delicious scent of green leaves, of full-blown roses, of dewy mosses; the air is damp and warm, he can hear the feet of the blackbirds scraping and turning over the mould and the grass; it is dark, yet he can distinguish the masses of the great woods beyond the gardens, the outlines of the trees near his casement, the shape of the clouds as they move slowly southward.

He wonders in what part of the old house, whose fantastic roofs and turrets, and gargoyles and ivy coloured buttresses are hidden in the dusk of the summer night, they have given the Princess Sabaroff her chamber. He remains some time at the open window, and goes to his bed as the dawn grows rosy.

" Lord Brandolin is in a very bad temper," says Mr. Wootton, when the smoking-room door has closed on the object of his detestation ; then he pauses, and adds significantly : " The Brandolins, you know, were always a little—just a little—clever family, very clever, but we all know to what great wits are sadly often allied. And this man has never done anything with all his talent and opportunities ; never done anything at all ?"

" He has written first-rate books !" says Usk, angrily, always ready to defend a friend in absence.

"Oh, books!" says Mr. Wootton, with bland but unutterable disdain. Mr. Wootton is a critic of books, and therefore naturally despises them.

"What would you have him do?" growls Usk, pugnaciously.

Mr. Wootton stretches his legs out, and gazes with abstracted air at the ceiling. "Public life," he murmurs. "Public life is the only possible career for an Englishman of position. But it demands sacrifices, it demands sacrifices."

"You mean that one has to marry?" says the young Duke of Whitby, timidly.

Mr. Wootton smiles on him loftily. "Marry! Yes, undoubtedly; and avoid scandals afterwards; avoid, beyond all, those connections which lend such a charm to existence, but are so apt to get into the newspapers!"

There is a general laugh.

Mr. Wootton has not intended to make

them laugh, and he resumes with stateliness, as though they had not interrupted him, " The country expects those sacrifices ; no man succeeds in public life in England who does not make them."

" Melbourne, Palmerston, Sydney Herbert surely didn't make 'em?" murmurs one rebellious hearer.

Mr. Wootton waves him aside, as he would do an importunate fly : " Not to touch on living persons, I would select Lord Althorp as the model of the public leader most suited to this country. It would not suit Lord Brandolin to lead the blameless life of a Lord Althorp. It would not suit him even to pretend to lead it. I doubt if he could even look the part, if he tried. The English are a peculiar people ; they always mix public and private life together. Lord Beaconsfield remarked to me once——"

And Mr. Wootton tells a story of Disraeli,

a very good story, only he has taken it out of the journals of the President des Brosses and fathered it on to Disraeli. But M. le President des Brosses is an author seldom read now, and nobody knows; if they did, nobody would care.

"Public opinion," he resumes, "is irresistible in England, and if it once turn against a man, were he Messiah himself, he could do nothing. It is not an intelligent public opinion; it confuses public and private qualifications. A man may be a great statesman, and yet dislike his wife, and like somebody else's. A man may be a great hero, and yet he may have an unseemly passion, or an unpaid tailor. But the British public does not understand this. It invariably overlooks the man's greatness, and only sees the lady or the tailor who compromises him. It thinks, unhappily or happily as you may choose to consider, that genius should keep the whole ten commandments. Now, genius is conspicuous for breaking them."

Mr. Wootton here knocks a little ash off his cigar, and smiles like a man who has said something neatly.

"It is the first time I ever heard you compliment genius," murmurs Lawrence Hamilton.

"In Italy," pursues Mr. Wootton, "not very long ago, a minister was accused of buying a piano out of the public funds for his mistress. Neither the piano nor the malversation hurt the gentleman in public estimation in that soft and accommodating clime. But that piano, though he might have paid for it with his own money, would have ruined an English politician. Though it had been the very smallest cottage piano conceivable, it would have buried him for ever under it if it had got talked about; he would never have explained it away, or made it even contingently endurable to the nation. You may, if you are a public man in England, commit every conceivable blunder, add millions to the National Debt, eat your own words every evening in debate, and plunge the country into an abyss of unmeasured and unmeasurable revolution, and they will still have confidence in you if you read the lessons in church and walk home with your wife : but, if it is ever rumoured that you admire your neighbour's wife, down you go for ever. And yet," continues Mr. Wootton, pensively, "people *do* admire their neighbour's wife in England, and it seems a venial offence when one compares it with the desertion of Gordon, or the encouragement of a hydra-headed greed for the rich man's goods."

With which Mr. Wootton yawns, rises, and also declares his intention to go to bed.

The young Duke follows him and walks

by his side down the corridor. He is not at all like Disraeli's young duke ; he is awkward, shy, and dull, he is neither amiable nor distinguished, but he has a painstaking wish in him to do well by his country, which is almost noble in a person who has been toadied, indulged, and tempted in all ways and on all sides ever since his cradle days. It is the disinterested patriotism which has been so largely the excellence and honour of the English nobility, and which is only possible in men of position so high that they are raised by it from birth above all vulgar jealousies or demagogue's greeds.

"Do you really think ? " says the Duke, timidly, for he is very afraid of Henry Wootton, "do you really think that to have any influence on English public life it is necessary—necessary—to keep so very straight, as regards women, I mean, you know ? "

"It is most necessary to *appear* to keep very straight," replies Mr. Wootton.

The two things are obviously different to the meanest capacity.

The young man sighs.

"And to have that—that—appearance, one must be married?"

"Indisputably. Marriage is as necessary to respectability in any great position as a brougham to a doctor, or a butler to a bishop. It is like a judge's wig: the wig is absurd, tiresome, stifling, but it imposes on the public and must be worn," replies the elder, smiling compassionately at the wick of his candle. He does not care a straw about the Duke, he has no daughters to marry, and Mr. Wootton's social eminence is far beyond the power of dukes or princes to make or mend.

"But," stammers his Grace of Whitby, growing red, yet burning with a desire for instruction, "but don't you think a—a connection with—with any lady of one's own rank is quite safe, quite sure not to cause scandal?"

Mr. Wootton balances his candlestick carefully on one finger, pauses in his walk, and looks hard at his questioner.

"*That would depend entirely upon the lady's temper*," replies this wise monitor of youth.

They are words of wisdom so profound, that they sink deep into the soul of his pupil, and fill him with a consternated sadness and perplexity.

The temper of Lady Dolgelly is a known quantity, and the quality of it is alarming. Lady Dolgelly is not young, she is goodlooking, and she has debts. Lord Dolgelly has, indeed, hitherto let her pay her debts in any way she chose, being occupied enough with paying such of his own as he cannot by any dexterity avoid; but there is no knowing what he may do any

day out of caprice or ill-nature, and although
he will never obtain a divorce, he may try
for one, which will equally effectually con-
vulse the Duke's county, and the Cathedral
city which is situated in its centre. His
own affair with Lady Dolgelly is, he firmly
believes, known to no human being save
themselves and their confidential servants;
he little dreams that it has been the gossip
of all London, until London grew tired of
it; he is, indeed, aware that everybody
invites them in the kindest manner together,
but he attributes this coincidence to her
tact in the management of her set and
choice of her own engagements.

The human mind is like the ostrich, its
own projects serve to it the purpose which
sand plays to the ostrich; comfortably
buried in them it defies the scrutiny of
mankind; wrapt in its own absorbing
passions it leaves its hansom before a
lady's hall door, or leaves its coroneted

handkerchief on a bachelor's couch, and never dreams that the world is looking on round the corner or through the key-hole. Human nature, the moment it is interested, becomes blind. Therefore, the Duke has put his question in all good faith.

He would abhor any kind of scandal He is devoted to his mother, who is a pious and very proper person ; he has a conscientious sense of his own vast duties and responsibilities ; he would feel most uncomfortable if he thought people were talking grossly of him in his own county ; and he has a horror of Lord Dolgelly, noisy, insolent, coarse, a gambler, and a rake.

Arrived at his bedroom door, Mr. Wootton is touched vaguely with a kind feeling towards his humble interrogator, or with some other sentiment less kindly, it may be. He pauses, looks straight before

"That kind of connections are invariably dangerous, invariably," he remarks. "They have their uses, I admit, they have their uses ; they mould a man's manners when he is young, they enable him to acquire great insight into female character, they keep him out of the lower sorts of entanglements, and they are useful in restraining him from premature marriage. But they are perilous if allowed to last too long. If permitted to claim privileges, rights, usurpations, they are apt to become irksome and compromising, especially if the lady be no longer young. When a woman is no longer young there is a desperate *acharnement* in her tenacity about a last passion which is like that of the mariner clinging to a spar in the midst of a gusty sea. It is not easy for the spar to disengage itself. On the whole, therefore, women of rank are, perhaps, best avoided in this sense. Passions are safest which can be terminated by the cheque-book. The cheque-book is not always, indeed, refused by great ladies—when they are in debt—but a cheque-book is an unpleasant witness in the law courts. However, as I said before, all depends on the lady's temper ; no woman who has a bad temper is ever truly discreet. Good-night to your Grace," and Mr. Wootton with his candle disappears within his doorway.

He smiles a little blandly as his man undresses him. Five years before, Lady Dolgelly offended him at a house party at Sandringham, taking a fiendish pleasure in capping all his best stories, and tracing the sources of all his epigrams. In that inaccessible but indelible note - book, his memory, he has written her name down as that of one to whom he has a debt to pay. "*Je lui ai donné du fil à retordre,*" he thinks, as he drops into his first doze.

CHAPTER VIII.

"ALAN is really coming to-morrow!" says
Dorothy Usk to her lord, with pleasure,
a few days later, looking up from a
telegram.

"How you excite yourself!" says Usk,
with rude disdain. "What can you see
in him to care about? He is a pretentious
humbug, if ever there was one!"

"George!" She regards him with horror
and amaze. Is he wholly out of his mind?
Her cousin is Lady Usk's ideal of what
an English gentleman should be. *He* does
not keep black women down in Warwickshire.

"A pretentious humbug," repeats Usk.
He likes to ticket his relations and con-

nections with well-chosen descriptions. "All good looks and soft sawder; women like that sort of thing——"

"Of course, we like good manners, though they are not your weakness," interrupts his wife, with acerbity. "Alan has the manners of a man who respects women; that may seem very tame to you and your friend Brandolin, but in these days it has at least the charm of novelty."

"Respects women!" Usk is unable to restrain his hilarity. "My dear Dolly, you're not a chicken, you can't mean that you don't know that Gervase——"

"I know that he is well-bred. You were so once, but it is a very long time ago," replies his wife, with cutting sententiousness, and with that unkind reply she leaves him. As if she did not understand men better than he, she thinks, contemptuously. He may understand dogs and horses, and deer and partridges, but about human nature he knows no more than the old man at the lodge gates.

"Surely she can't be soft on Gervase herself," her husband reflects, with a sensation of amusement; "it would be too funny after running so straight all these years, and just as her daughters are growing up—but they often are like that."

He is not sure whether the idea diverts or irritates him, but he knows that he has always detested Gervase, such a coxcomb and such a humbug as the fellow is!

"Respect women, good Lord!" ejaculated Usk in his solitude.

"To be sure," adds that honest gentleman in his own mind, "there are very few of 'em who would thank you to respect 'em now-a-days."

"Gervase will be here to-morrow," he says in the course of the day to Princess Sabaroff.

" Indeed," she replies, with indifference, " who is he ?"

" A friend of my wife's ; at least a cousin ; I thought you might know him ; he was some time in Russia."

"No." There is a coldness in the negative disproportioned to so simple a denial. " I do not think so. I do not remember such a name. Who is he ?"

" A person who is expected to be great in foreign affairs some day or another," says Brandolin. " He will have one qualification rare in an English foreign minister; daily growing rarer, thanks to the imbecilities of examinations; he knows how to bow and he knows what to say."

" A friend of yours ?"

" Oh, no ; an acquaintance. He thinks very ill of me."

" Why ?"

" Because I do nothing for my country. He thinks he does a great deal when he

"That is not generous. The world owes much to diplomatists, it will know how much in a few years, when it will be governed by clerks, controlled by telephones."

"That is true; I stand corrected. But Gervase and I have few sympathies; none, indeed, except politically, and even there we differ—his is the Toryism of Peel, mine is the Toryism of Pitt—there are leagues between the two."

"I know: the one is Opportunism; the other is Optimate-ism."

"Perhaps," says Brandolin.

"Does she know Gervase, despite her denial?" he wonders. He has an impression that she does. There was a look of recognition in her eyes when she gave that vague, bland gesture in answer to her host. All trifles in her interest him, as they always do interest a man in a woman whom he admires, and is not sure that he understands ; and Gervase, he is aware, has been a good deal in Russia.

He himself has known the subject of their discourse ever since they were boys, and had that sort of intimacy with him which exists between men who live in the same sets and belong to the same clubs. But to him, Gervase seems a *petit maître*, a *poseur*, a man artificial, conventional, ambitious in small things, and to Gervase, he himself seems much as he does to Lady Usk, a perverse and lawless Bohemian, only saved from the outer darkness by the fact of his aristocratic birth.

Meanwhile, in her own room, Xenia Sabaroff is pursuing her own reflections whilst her maid disrobes her.

"It will be better to see him once and for all," she muses. "I cannot go on for ever avoiding him in every city in Europe.

Very likely he will not even remember my face or my name!"

She feels a strong temptation to invent some plausible reason and break off her visit to Surrenden; but she is a courageous woman, and flight is repugnant to her. More than once of late she has avoided a meeting which is disagreeable to her by some abrupt change of her own plans or reversal of her own engagements. To continue to do this seems weakness. Indeed, to do it at all seems too great a flattery to the person avoided. What is painful is best encountered without procrastination. It is the old question of grasping the nettle.

A haughty flush passes over her face at her own reflections. After all, to have any emotion at all about it, pleasurable or painful, is equally an humiliation. She is a proud woman, as well as a courageous one. There are memories associated with

hateful.

Women like Mrs. Wentworth Curzon carry such memories lightly, or rather do not carry them at all, but bury them by scores, pell-mell, one on the top of another like old letters, and forget all about their interment ; but she is different to them.

It has not been difficult for her to avoid meeting Lord Gervase : he is one of those persons whose movements are known and chronicled ; but she is conscious that the time is come when she can no longer escape doing so, except by such an abrupt departure that it would seem to herself too great a weakness, and be to him too great a flattery, for such a step to enter for an instant into the category of possibilities. It is, she reflects, or it should be, a matter to her of absolute indifference to see again a person whom she has not seen for seven years.

Yet she is conscious of a sense of pain
and excitation as her woman puts on her a
maize satin tea-gown, covered with point
d'Alençon, at five o'clock the next day, and
she knows that when she goes down to
the tea-room in a few minutes Gervase,
who was to arrive by the afternoon train,
will in all probability be present there.

Everyone is indoors that day, for a fine
summer rain is falling without, and has
been falling since noon. All the house
party are in the library, and the children
are there also; the windows are open, and
the sweet smell from the damp gardens and
wet grass fills the air.

Everyone is laughing and talking; Usk
is drinking a glass of Kummel, and Brandolin is playing with the dog; conversing
with Nina Curzon and the mistress of the
house, and standing in front of them, is a
tall, fair man, irreproachable in *tenue*, and
extremely distinguished in appearance. He

is Lord Gervase. His back is towards the door, and he does not see or hear her enter, but as the Babe rushes towards her, toppling over a stool and treading mercilessly on the trains of tea-gowns in the wind of his going, the noise made by the child makes him turn his head, and an expression of recognition, mingled with amazement, passes over his usually impassive features.

"Is that not Princess Sabaroff?" he asks of his hostess, with a certain breathless astonishment betrayed in his voice.

Lady Usk assents. "One of my dearest friends," she adds. "I think you don't know her? I will present you in a moment. She is as clever as she is beautiful. The children adore her. Look at Babe."

The Babe has dragged his Princess to a couch and climbed up on it himself, kneeling half on her lap and half off it, with no respect for the maize satin, whilst his impatient little feet beat the devil's tatoo amongst the point d'Alençon.

"My dear Babe, do not be such a monopolist," said Brandolin, as he approaches with a cup of tea and a wafer of caviare bread and butter. "Your shoes have seventeenth-century buckles, it is true, yet still they are scarcely *bibelots* to be wrapped up in a lady's dress."

The Babe grins saucily, tossing his hair out of his eyes; but with unwonted obedience he disentangles his feet with some care out of the lace.

Xenia Sabaroff does not take as much notice of him as usual. She is reserved and pre-occupied. Brandolin, like the child, fails in awakening her interest or attention. She has seated herself almost with her back to where Gervase is standing, but every now and then she looks half-round as by an irresistible, unconscious impulse of curiosity.

Brandolin notes the gesture, as her actions have an interest for him which grows daily in its fascination. "There is Dorothy Usk's Phœnix," he says to her in a low tone, when the Babe has scampered off after bon-bons; he indicates Gervase with a glance. Her eyebrows contract slightly, as in some displeasure or constraint.

"Lady Usk is very soon satisfied," she replies, coldly. "Her own amiability makes her see perfection everywhere."

"It is a quality we cannot value too highly in so imperfect a world. It is better than seeing everything *en noir*, surely?" says Brandolin. "If we make people what we think them, as optimists say, it is best to be optimistic."

"I dislike optimism," she says, curtly. "It is absurd and untrue. Our Dostoievsky is a wiser novelist than your Dickens. Yet one is so weak, one must believe something."

"It is pretty for a woman to think so,"

says Brandolin, "but myself, I have never seen why. I may hope, I may wish, I may regret, I may—if I am very sanguine, even expect; but believe—no!"

"Perhaps I should like to believe in a woman," he adds, more softly, with that inflection of his voice which has always had, at all events, the effect of making women believe in him.

Madame Sabaroff is not so easily touched as many. She pauses a moment, then says with a certain weariness, "Anybody who can believe can love; that is nothing new."

"What would be new? To love and disbelieve in what we love? It would be very painful."

"It would be a test," says his companion.

Then she drops the subject decidedly by approaching the other ladies. Brandolin has a faint sense of discomfiture and sadness; he is accustomed to very facile conquests; and yet he is not a coxcomb like Lawrence Hamilton; he does not precisely anticipate one here, but habit is second nature, and it has been his habit to succeed with women with rapidity and ease. That sense of mystery which there is also for him in the Princess Xenia oppresses whilst it allures him. He is English enough to think that he dislikes mystery, yet, as an element of romance, it has always an irresistible fascination for romantic temperaments.

Gervase, meanwhile, has sunk into a chair by the side of Nina Curzon, and is saying in a whisper, "Who is that lady? The one with her back to us, to whom Lord Brandolin is so *empressé?* I thought I knew all the Usks' people."

"Look in your Russian memories, and you will probably find that you know her too," replies Mrs. Curzon.

"Oh, she is Russian?" says Gervase,

then adds, negligently, "I think, now you tell me that, I have seen her before. Is she not the Princess Sabaroff?"

"Why did you pretend not to know her," thinks Nina Curzon, as she answers: "Yes, that is her name. You must have met her in Petersburg."

"Petersburg is very dim in my memories," he replies, evasively. "Its baccarat is what made the deepest impression on my remembrance and my fortunes. Now I think of it, however, I recollect her quite well; her husband was Anatole Sabaroff, and Lustoff shot him in a duel about her? Am I right?"

"So charming for her," says Nina Curzon. "Englishwomen never have anything happen for them picturesque like that; our men always die of indigeston or going after a fox."

" How one comes across people."

"'After long years,'" quotes Mrs. Curzon, with mock romance in her tones. 'Generally, I think," she adds, with a little yawn, "we can never get rid of our people, the world is so small, and there is really only one set in it that is decent, so we can't ever get out of it. It must have been very nice in Romeo and Juliet's days when a little drive to Mantua took you into realms wholly inaccessable to your Verona acquaintances. Now-a-days, if you run away from anybody in London, you are sure to run against them in Yeddo or Yucatan."

" Constancy made easy, like the three R's," says Gervase. " Unfortunately, despite our improved facilities, we are not constant."

" He means to imply that he threw over the Sabaroff," thinks Mrs. Curzon, " but he is such a boaster of his *bonnes fortunes*

lying."

"Pray let me make you known to Madame Sabaroff," says Lady Usk to him a little later. "She is such a very dear friend of mine, and I see you have been looking at her ever since she entered the room."

"She is a very handsome person; any one would look at her," replies her cousin. Were he not so perfectly well-bred and impassive, it might almost be said that the suggested presentation fills him with some vague nervousness.

Nina Curzon watches him inquisitively as he is led up and presented to Madame Sabaroff.

rassed.

Brandolin, playing with the collie dog near at hand, listens and observes.

Lady Usk is not so observant. "It is a long time since he was in Russia," she says to her friend, "I daresay you have forgotten; his father was alive and his name was Baird, then, you know."

Xenia Sabaroff makes a little polite gesture expressive of entire indifference to the change in these titles. With an action which would be rude in any woman less high-bred, she turns away her head and speaks to Brandolin, ignoring the acquaintance and the presence of Gervase.

Across the good-natured and busy brain of her hostess there flashes an electric and odious thought; is it possible that Usk may be right, and that there may be something wrong after all in this her latest and most adored friend?   She feels that she will die of suffocated curiosity if she do not speedily get her cousin alone, and learn all he has ever known or heard of the Princess Sabaroff.

"A snub direct!" whispers Lawrence Hamilton to Mr. Wootton.

"Or a cut direct; which?" says that far-sighted gentleman.

"Anyhow, it's delightful to see him let in for it," reflects Usk, who has also observed the incident from where he stands by the liqueurs.

Gervase, who has never been known to be at a loss in any position, however difficult, colours, and looks at once annoyed and confused.   He stands before Xenia Sabaroff for a few moments hesitating and irresolute, conscious that everyone is looking at him; then he takes refuge with Lady Dawlish, whom he detests, because she is the nearest person to him.

"Madame Sabaroff is eclipsing the black women," says that lady.

"What black women?" asks Gervase, very inattentive and bored. She tells him the story of the Hindoo harem and he hears no word of it.

"Brandolin is always so odd," he says, indifferently, watching the hand of Xenia Sabaroff as it rests on the shoulder of the Babe who is leaning against her knees gazing at her adoringly.

"Why did you pretend not to know her?" says Mrs. Curzon to him.

He smiles the fatuous smile with which a man ingeniously expresses what he would be thought a brute to put into words.

"She does not deign to know me—now," he says, modestly and to the experienced comprehension of Nina Curzon, the words, although so modest, tell her as much as the loudest boast could do.

Gervase is angered, irritated, interested

and mortified all at once. He has never been in an absurd position before, and he is aware that he was in one a moment ago, and that the whole house party of Surrenden Court saw him in it. "What a fool Dolly was not to tell me she was here," he thinks, forgetting that his cousin and hostess has not the remotest suspicion that he and the Princess Xenia have ever met each other before.

"Seven years!" he thinks. "Good Heavens, what an eternity! And she is handsomer than she was then; very handsome; wonderfully handsome."

He looks at her all the while from under his half-closed eyelids, whilst he talks he knows not what kind of rubbish to Lady Dawlish.

Xenia Sabaroff does not once look his way. The moment which she had dreaded has passed, and it has made no impression whatever upon her; her indifference reconciles her to herself. Is it possible, she wonders, that she ever loved, or ever thought that she loved, this man?

Throughout that evening he does not venture to approach her again, and he endeavours to throw himself with some show of warmth into a flirtation with Nina Curzon.

CHAPTER IX.

GERVASE saunters into his hostess's boudoir the next morning, availing himself of the privilege accorded to that distant relationship which it pleases them both to raise into an intimate cousinship. It is a charming boudoir, style Louis Quinze, with the walls hung with flowered silk of that epoch, and the dado made of fans which belonged to the same period. Lady Usk writes here at a little secretaire, painted by Fragonard, and uses an inkstand, said to have belonged to Madame de Parabère, made in the shape of a silver shell, driven by a gold Cupidon; yet, despite the frivolity of these associations, she contrives to get through a vast

experiences.

She is used to being the confidante of her men; she is young enough to make a friend who is attractive to them, and old enough to lend herself *de bon cœur* to the recital of their attachments to other women. Very often she gives them very good advice, but she does not obtrude it unseasonably. "An awfully nice woman all round," is the general verdict of her visitants to the boudoir. She does not seek to be more than that to them.

Gervase does not make any confidences; he only tells her things which amuse her and reveal much about her acquaintances, nothing about himself. He smokes some of her favourite cigarettes, praises some new china, suggests an alteration in the arrangement of the fans, and makes critical discourses *apropos* of her collection of snuff-boxes.

When he is going away, he lingers a moment, intently looking at a patch box of vernis Martin, and says, with studied carelessness: "Dolly, tell me, when did you make the acquaintance of Madame Sabaroff?"

"Last year, at Cannes; why do you want to know? She came and stayed with us at Orme last Easter. Is she not perfectly charming?"

"Very good-looking," says Gervase, absently. "You don't know anything about her, then?"

"Know?" repeats his hostess. "What should I know? What everybody does, I suppose. I met her first at the Duchess de Luynes. You can't possibly mean that there can be anything—anything——"

"Oh, no," replies Gervase, but it produces on his questioner the same effect as if he had said "Oh, yes."

"How odious men are! Such scandal-mongers," says Lady Usk, angrily. "Talk of *our* 'damning with faint praise!' There is nothing comparable to the way in which a man destroys a woman's reputation just by raising his eyebrows or twisting his moustache!"

"I have no moustache to twist, and am sure there is no reputation which I wish to destroy," says her cousin.

"Then why do you ask me where I made her acquaintance?"

"My dear Dolly! Surely the most innocent and general sort of question ever on the lips of any human being!"

"Possibly; not in the way you said it, however, and when one knows that you were a great deal in Russia, it suggests five hundred things—five thousand things

—and of course one knows he was shot in a duel about her, and I believe people have talked."

" I have never helped them to talk. When do they not talk?"

And beyond this she cannot prevail upon him to go. He pretends that the Princess Sabaroff is beyond all possibility of any approach to calumny, but the protestation produces on her the impression that he could tell her a great deal wholly to the contrary if he chose.

" She certainly was staying with Madame de Luynes," she insists.

" Whoever said the lady might not stay with the Archbishop of Canterbury?" replies Gervase.

She is irritated and vexed.

Xenia Sabaroff is her idol of the moment, and if her idol were proved human she would be very angry. She reflects that she will have Dodo and the children kept more strictly in the school-room, and not let them wander about over the park as they do with their Russian friend most mornings.

"One can never be too careful with children of that age," she muses, "and they are terribly *cvillées* already."

Dorothy Usk's friendships, though very ardent, are like most friendships which exist in society; they are apt to blow about with every breeze. She is cordial, kind, and in her way sincere; but she is what her husband characterises as "weather-cocky."

Who is not "weathercocky" in the world?

Although so tolerant in appearance of naughty people, because it is the fashion to be so, and not to be so looks priggish, and dowdy, and odd, she never, at the bottom of her heart, likes her naughty people. She has run very straight herself.

as her lord would express it; she has been always much too busy to have time or inclination to be tempted " off the rails," and she has little patience with women who have gone off them; only she never says so, because it would look so goody-goody and stupid, and for fear of looking so she even manages to stifle in her own breast her own antipathy to Dulcia Waverley.

There have been very many martyrs to the sense that they ought to smile at virtue when they hate it, but Dorothy Usk's martyrdom is of a precisely opposite kind, she forces herself to seem to approve the reverse of virtue whilst she detests it. Anything is better, in her creed, than looking odd; and now-a-days you do look so odd and so old-fashioned if you make a fuss about anything. Still, in her heart of hearts, she feels excessively vexed, because it is quite apparent to her that

Gervase knows something very much to the disadvantage of her new acquaintance.

"George will be so delighted if he finds out that Madame Sabaroff is like all those horrid women he is so fond of," she reflects. " I shall never hear the last of it from him. It will be a standing joke for him the whole of his life."

Certainly, Madame Sabaroff is letting Brandolin carry on with her more than is altogether proper. True, they are people who may marry each other, if they please, but Brandolin is not a man who marries, and his attentions are never likely to take that form. He probably pays so much court to Madame Sabaroff because he has heard that of her which leads him to suppose that his efforts may be *couronné*, as French vaudevillists say, without any thought of marriage.

Lady Usk has always known he is horribly unprincipled : more so than even

subjects.

"What's the row, my lady, you look ruffled?" inquires Usk, coming into her boudoir with a sheaf of half-opened letters in his hand.

"There are always things to annoy one," she answers, vaguely.

"It is an arrangement of a prudential Providence to prevent our affections being set on this world," replies Usk, piously.

His wife's only comment on this religious declaration is an impatient twist to the tail of her Maltese dog.

Usk proceeds to turn over to her such letters as bore him; they are countable by dozens; the two or three which interest him have been read in the gun-room and put away in an inside pocket.

"Mr. Bruce could attend to all these,"

she says, looking with some disgust at the correspondence. Bruce is his secretary.

" He always blunders," says Usk.

" Then change him," says his wife; nevertheless she is pleased at the compliment implied to herself.

" All secretaries are fools," says Usk, impartially.

" Even Secretaries of State," says Mr. Wootton, who has the entrée of the boudoir, and saunters in at that moment. " I have some news this morning," he adds : " Coltsfoot marries Miss Hoard."

" Never!" exclaims Dorothy Usk.

" Perfectly true," says Mr. Wootton. " Both of them staying at Dunrobin, and engagement publicly announced."

Lord Coltsfoot is heir to a dukedom ; Miss Hoard is the result, in bullion, of ironworks.

" Never!" reiterates Lady Usk. " It is impossible that he can do such a horrible thing ! Why, she has one shoulder higher than the other and red eyes."

" There are six millions paid down," replies Mr. Wootton, sententiously.

" What the deuce will Mrs. Donnington say ?" asks Usk.

"One never announces any marriage," remarks Mr. Wootton, "but there is a universal outcry about what will some lady, married long ago to somebody else, say to it. Curious result of supposed monogamy ?"

" It is quite disgusting !" says Lady Usk. " Some of those new people are presentable, but she isn't, and Coltsfoot is so good-looking and so young."

" It is what the French call an '*alliance très comme il faut*,'" says Usk, from sheer spirit of contradiction. " The duke-dom is as full of holes as an old tin pot ; she tinkers it up with her iron and gold ; and I bet you that your friend Worth will manage to cut Lady Coltsfoot's gowns so that one shoulder higher than the other will become all the rage next season."

"Of course, you set no store on such a simple thing as happiness," says his wife, with acerbity.

"Happiness? Lord, my dear! Happiness was buried with Strephon and Chloe centuries ago! We are amused or bored; we are successful or unsuccessful; we are popular or unpopular; we are somebody or we are nobody; but we are never either happy or miserable."

"People who have a heart are still both!"

"A heart! You mean spoons!"

"What a hideous expression! Strephon and Chloe never used that."

"When we have an unfortunate passion now," remarks Mr. Wootton, "we go to Karlsbad. It's only an affair of the liver."

"Or the nerves," suggests Usk. "Flirtation is the proper thing, flirtation never hurts anybody; it's like puff paste, seltzer water, and Turkish cigarettes."

"Puff paste may bring on an indigestion when one's too old to eat it!"

"There! Didn't I tell you so? She's always saying something about my age. 'A man is the age that he feels.'"

"No, 'a woman is the age that she looks.' If you will quote things, quote them properly."

"The age that she looks? That's so very variable. She's twenty when she enters a ballroom at midnight; she's fifty when she comes out at sunrise; she's sixteen when she goes to meet somebody at Hurlingham; she's sixty when she scolds her maid and has a scene with her husband!"

Lady Usk interrupts him with vivacity:

"And he? Pray isn't he five-and-twenty when he's in Paris alone, and five-and-ninety when he's grumbling at home?"

" Because he's bored at home! Youth is, after all, only good spirits. If you laugh you are young, but your wife don't make you laugh. You pay her bills and go with her to a State ball, and sit opposite to her at dinner, and when you catch a cold she is always there to say, ' My dear, didn't I tell you so?' but I defy any man living to recall any hour of his existence in which his wife ever made him feel lively!"

" And yet you wanted me to ask married people together!"

" Because I wanted it all to be highly proper and deadly dull. Surrenden has got a sort of reputation of being a kind of Orleans Club."

" And yet you complain of being bored in it!"

" One is always bored in one's own house! One can never take in to dinner the person one likes."

"You make up to yourself for the deprivation after dinner!"

"My lady's very ruffled to-day," says Usk to Mr. Wootton. "I don't know which of her doves has turned out a fighting cock."

"That reminds me," observes Mr. Wootton. "I wanted to ask you, did you know that Gervase, when he was Lord Baird, was very much *au mieux* with Madame Sabaroff? I remember hearing long ago from Russians——"

Lady Usk interrupts the great man angrily:

"Very much *au mieux!* What barbarous polyglot language for a great critic like you! Must you have the assistance of bad grammar in two tongues to take away my friend's reputation?"

Lord Usk chuckles.

"Reputations aren't taken away so easily; they're very hardy plants now-a-days, and will stand a good deal of bad weather!"

Mr. Wootton is shocked.

"Oh, dearest Lady Usk! Reputation! You couldn't think I meant to imply of any guest of yours—only, you know, he was secretary in Petersburg when he was Lord Baird, and so—and so——"

"Well! It does not follow that he is the lover of every woman in Petersburg!"

Mr. Wootton is infinitely distressed.

"Oh, indeed! I didn't mean anything of that sort."

"You did mean everything of that sort," murmurs his hostess.

"But, you see, he admired her very much, was constantly with her, and yesterday I saw they don't speak to each other, so I was curious to know what could be the reason."

"I believe she didn't recognise him."

Mr. Wootton smiles.

"Oh! ladies have such prodigious powers of oblivion—and remembrance!"

"Yes," observes Usk, with complacency;
"the storms of memory sometimes sink into
them as if they were sponges, and sometimes glide off them as if they were ducks.
It is just as they find it convenient."

"But Madame Sabaroff can't have been
more than a child when Gervase was in
Russia," cries Lady Usk.

Mr. Wootton smiles again significantly.

"She was married."

"To a brute!"

"All husbands," says Usk, with another
chuckle, "are brutes, and all wives are
angels. *C'est imprimé.*"

"I hope no one will ever call me an
angel; I should know at once that I was
a bore!"

"My dear Alan," says Dorothy Usk, having got him at a disadvantage in her boudoir a quarter-of-an-hour after this discussion. "What has there been between you and the Princess Sabaroff? Everybody feels there is something. It is in the air. Indeed, everybody is talking about it. Pray tell me! I am dying to know."

Gervase is silent.

"Everybody in the house is sure of it," continues his hostess. "They don't say so, of course, but they think so. Nina Curzon, who is *mauvaise langue*, pretends even that she knows all the circumstances, and it would seem that they are not very nice circumstances. I really cannot consent to go on in the dark any longer."

"Ask the lady," replies Gervase, stiffly.

"I certainly shall do nothing so ill-bred. You are a man, you are a relation of mine; and I can say things to you I couldn't possibly say to a stranger, which Madame Sabaroff is quite to me. If you won't answer, I shall only suppose that you paid court to her and were 'spun,' as the boys say at the examinations."

"Not at all," says Gervase, haughtily.

"Then tell me the story."

He hesitates. "I don't know whether you will think very well of me if I tell you the truth."

"That you may be sure I shall not. No man ever behaves well where women are in the question."

"My dear Dolly! what unkind exaggeration! If I tell you anything, you will be sure not to repeat what I say? Madame Sabaroff considers me a stranger to her; I am bound to accept her decision on such a point."

"You knew her in Russia?"

"Yes; when I was there she was the new beauty at the Court. She had been married a year or less to Anatole Sabaroff. I had the honour of her friendship at that time ; if she withdraws it now I must acquiesce."

" Oh !"

Lady Usk gives a little sound between a snort and a sigh.

She is annoyed. The gossipers are right then. She is sorry the children have been so much with their friend, and she is infuriated at the idea of her husband's triumph over her credulity.

" Oh, pray don't think—don't think for a moment," murmurs Gervase, but his cousin understands that it is the conventional compulsory expostulation which every man who is well-bred is bound to make on such subjects.

" She must have been very young then ?" she says, beating impatiently on her blotting-book with her gold pen.

" Very young ; but such a husband as

Anatole Sabaroff made is—well—a more than liberal education to any woman, however young. She was sixteen, I think, and very lovely, though she is perhaps handsomer now. I had the honour of her confidence, she was unhappy and *incomprise;* her father had given her hand in discharge of a debt at cards; Sabaroff was a gambler and a brute; at the end of the second winter season he had a violent fit of jealousy and sent her to his estate on the White Sea——"

"Jealousy of you?"

Gervase bowed.

"Where she was kept in a state of surveillance scarcely better than absolute imprisonment. I did all manner of crazy and romantic things to endeavour to see her; and once or twice I succeeded, but he had discovered letters of mine and made her captivity more rigorous than ever. I myself was ordered on the special mission to Spain—you remember—and I left Russia with a broken heart. From that time to this I have never seen her."

"But your broken heart has continued to do its daily work?"

"It is a figure of speech. I adored her, and the husband was a brute. When Lustoff shot him he only rid the world of a brute. You have seen that broad bracelet she wears above the right elbow? People always talk so about it. She wears it to hide where Sabaroff broke her arm one night in his violence; the marks of it are there for ever."

Lady Usk is silent; she is divided between her natural compassion and sympathy, which are very easily roused, and her irritation at discovering that her new favourite is what Usk would call "just like all the rest of them."

"You perceive," he added, "that as the Princess chooses wholly to ignore the past, it is not for me to recall it. I am obliged to accept her decision, however much I must suffer from it."

"Suffer!" echoes his cousin. "After her husband's death you never took the trouble to cross Europe to see her?"

"Could not get away," says Gervase, but he feels that the excuse is a frail one. And how, he thinks angrily, should a good woman like his cousin, who has never flirted in her life, and never done anything which might not have been printed in the daily papers, understand a man's inevitable inconsistency.

"I assure you that I have never loved any woman as I loved her," he continues.

"Then you are another proof, if one were wanted, that men have died and worms have eaten them, but not for——"

"I did not die, certainly," Gervase says, much irritated, "But I suffered greatly, whether you choose to believe it or not."

"I am not inclined to believe it," replies his hostess. "It is not your style."

"I wrote to her a great many times." He pauses.

Lady Usk fills up the pause. "And she answered you?" she inquires.

"N-no," replies Gervase, unwilling to confess such an affront to him. "She did not write. Prudence, I suppose, or perhaps she might be too closely watched, or her letters might be stopped; who can say?"

"Nobody but herself, clearly. Well?"

"I was sent to Madrid; and I heard nothing of her except that Sabaroff was shot in a duel about her with Lustoff, but that was two years afterwards."

"And when he was shot, why did you not in due course go to the White Sea, or wherever she was, and offer yourself?"

"The truth is I had become acquainted with a Spanish lady——"

" A great many Spanish ladies, no doubt! What a half-hearted Lothario!"

" Not at all. Only just at that time——"

" Manillas, mandolines, balconies, bull-fights, high mass and moonlight had the supremacy! My dear Alan, tell your story how you will, you can't make yourself heroic."

" I have not the smallest pretension to do so!" says Gervase, very much annoyed. "I have no heroism. I leave it to Lord Brandolin, who has been shipwrecked five hundred times, I believe, and ridden as many dromedaries over unknown sand-plains as Gordon——"

" As you don't care in the least for her, why should you care if his shipwrecks and his dromedaries interest her? We don't know that they do, but——"

" How little sympathy you have!"

" George says I have always a great deal too much. What do you want me to sympathise with? According to your own story you 'loved and rode away;' at least, took a through ticket across Europe as Lovelace has to do in these prosaic days. If you did not go back to Russia when you might have gone back, *à qui la faute?* Nobody's but your own and the nameless Spanish lady or ladies'!"

"You are very perverse."

"It is you who are, or who were, perverse. According to your own story you adored a woman when she was unattainable; when she became attainable you did not even take the trouble to get into a railway carriage: you were otherwise amused. What romantic element is there in such a tale as yours to excite the smallest fragment of interest? To judge you out of your own mouth, you seem to have behaved with most uninteresting inconstancy."

"It was four years, and she had never answered my letters."

"Really a reason to make you esteem

her infinitely more than if she had answered them. My dear Alan, you were a flirt, and you forgot, as flirts forget: why should one pity you for being so comfortably and so easily consoled? You ought to be infinitely grateful that Madame Sabaroff did not send you reams of reproaches, and telegraph you compromising messages which would have got you into trouble in Downing-street. The thing died a natural death, you did not care to keep it alive; why are you now all lamentations over its grave? I really do not follow the course of your emotions— if you feel any emotion, I thought you never did. Madame Sabaroff has never been a person difficult to follow or to find; the fashionable intelligence of the newspapers would at any time have enabled you to know where she was; you never had inclination or remembrance enough to make you curious to see her again, and then when you come across her in a country house, you think yourself very ill-used because she does not all at once fall in your arms. You couldn't possibly care about her since you never tried to see her all those years!"

Dorothy Usk is really annoyed. She is not a person who has a high standard of humanity at any time, and she knows men thoroughly, and they have no chance of being heroes in her sight. But she likes a man to be a man, and to be an ardent lover, if he be a lover at all, and her favourite cousin seems to her to wear a poor aspect in this page of his autobiography.

"Pray did you know that she is as rich as she is?" she asks, with some sharpness in her tone.

Gervase colours a little, being conscious that his response cannot increase his cousin's sympathies with him.

"Not nonsense at all. Two years ago some silver was discovered on a bit of rough land which belonged to her, somewhere beyond the Urals, I think, and she is enormously rich, will be richer every year they say."

"Indeed!"

He endeavours to look indifferent, but his cousin's penetrating eyes seem to him to be reading his very soul.

"How dreadfully sorry he must be that he didn't leave Madrid," she thinks, and aloud says, irritably, "Why on earth didn't you try to renew things with her all these years?"

"I imagined that I had forgotten her."

"Well, so you had; completely for-gotten her, till you saw her here."

"On my honour, she is the only woman I have ever really loved."

"Oh, men always say that of somebody or another, generally of the most impossible people. George always declares that the only woman he ever really loved was a pastry - cook, when he was at Christ Church."

"Dear Dorothy, don't joke. I assure you I am thoroughly in earnest."

"She certainly has forgotten you."

She knows that for him to be convinced of this is the surest way to revive a died-out passion.

"Who knows? She would be indifferent in that case, and polite; as it is, she is cold, even rude."

"That may be resentment."

"Resentment means remembrance."

"Oh, not always."

"Then she has a number of my letters."

"So you said; you cannot be so very sure she has kept them. Other people may have written her the same sort of letters, or more admirable letters still; how can you tell?"

He colours angrily.

"She is not a *femme légère.*"

"She is receiving a great deal of attention now from Lord Brandolin, and she does not seem to dislike it. They say he writes exquisite letters to women he is fond of; I don't know myself, because I have never had anything more interesting from him than notes about dinners or visits, but they say so. They even say that his deserted ladies forgive his desertions because he writes his farewells so divinely."

"Lord Brandolin's epistolary accomplishments do not interest me in the least. Everybody knows what he is with women."

He pauses a moment; then adds, with some hesitation:

"Dear Dorothy, you know her very well. Don't you think you could find out for me, and tell me——"

"What?"

"Well, what she thinks or does not think; in a word, how I stand with her."

"No—oh, no, my dear Alan; I couldn't attempt anything of that sort; in my own house, too; it would seem so horribly rude. Besides, I am not in the least—not the very least—intimate with her. I think her charming; we are *bonnes connaissances*, the children adore her; but I have never said anything intimate to her in my life—never."

You can do it yourself if you want it done.
You are not usually shy."

Gervase gets up impatiently, and walks
about in the narrow limits of the boudoir
to the peril of the Sevrés and Saxe.

"But women have a hundred indirect
ways of finding out everything ; you
might discover perfectly well, if you chose,
whether—whether she feels angry or any
other sentiment ; whether—whether, in a
word, it would be prudent to recall the
past to her."

Lady Usk shakes her head with energy,
stirring all its pretty blonde curls, real
and false. "*Entre l'arbre et l'écorce ne
mettez pas le doigt.* That is sound advice
which I have heard given at the Français."

"That is said of not interfering between
married people."

"It is generally true of people who
wish, or may not wish, to marry. And I
suppose, Alan, that when you speak in my

house of renewing your—your—relations with the Princess Sabaroff, you do not mean that you have any object less serious than *le bon motif ?*"

Gervase is amused, although he is disconcerted and irritated.

"Come, Dolly, your guests are not always so very serious, are they? I never knew you so prim before."

Then she in turn feels angry. She always steadily adheres to the convenient fiction that she knows nothing whatever of the amorous filaments which bind her guests together in pairs, as turtle doves might be tied together by blue ribands.

"If you desire to re-awake the sentiments of Madame Sabaroff in your own favour, that you may again make sport of them, you must excuse me if I say that I cannot assist your efforts, and that I sincerely hope that they will not be successful," she says, with dignity and distance.

"Do you suppose his are any better than mine?" asks Gervase, irritably, as he waves his hand towards the window which looks on the west gardens. Between the yew and cedar trees, at some distance from the house, Brandolin is walking beside Xenia Sabaroff; his manner is interested and deferential, she moves with slow and graceful steps down the grassy paths, listening with apparent willingness; her head is uncovered, she carries a large sunshade opened over it made of white lace and pale rose silk; she has a cluster of Duchess of Sutherland roses in her hand. They are really only speaking of recent French poets, but those who look at them cannot divine that.

"He is not my cousin, and he does not solicit my assistance," says Dorothy Usk, seeing the figures in her garden with some displeasure. "*Je ne fais pas la police pour les autres;* but if he asked me what

irony.

"Probably," says his hostess, who is very skilful at fanning faint flame. "He is not a man whom I like myself, but many women, most women, I believe, think him irresistible."

Thereon she leaves him, without any more sympathy or solace, to go and receive some county people who have come to call, and who converse principally about prize poultry.

"*Comme elles sont assommates avec leurs poules!*" says the Marquise de Caillac, who chanced to be present at this infliction; and gazes in stupefaction at a Dowager-Duchess who has driven over from twenty miles off, who wears very thick boots, her own thin grey hair, waterproof tweed clothing, and a hat tied under her double chin with black strings. "*Un paquet !*" murmurs Marquise de Caillac, "*un veritable paquet !*"

"*C'est la vertu Anglaise, un peu démodeé,*" says Lord Iona, with a yawn.

Gervase stays on at Surrenden, somewhat bored, very much *enervé*, but fascinated too by the presence of his Russian Ariadne, and stung by the sight of Brandolin's attentions to her into such a strong sense of revived passion, that he means what he says when he declares to his cousin that the wife of Sabaroff was the only woman he has ever really loved. Her manner to him also, not cold enough to be complimentary, but entirely indifferent, never troubled, never moved in any way by his vicinity or by his direct allusions to the past, is such as irritates, piques, attracts and magnetises him. It seems to him incredible that any woman can ignore him so utterly. If she only seemed afraid of him, agitated in any way, even adversely, he could understand what was passing in her mind, but he cannot even flatter himself that she does this; she treats him with just such perfect indifference as she shows to the Duke of Whitby or Hugo Mountjoy, or any one of the gilded youths there present. If he could once see a wistful memory in her glance, once see a flush of colour on her face at his approach, it is probable that his vanity would be satisfied, and his interest cease as quickly as it has revived; but he never does see anything of this sort, and, by the rule of contradiction, his desire to see it increases. And he wonders uneasily what she has done with his letters.

CHAPTER X.

Lord Gervase was eight years younger when he wrote those letters, than he is now, and he has unpleasant recollections of unpleasant passages in them which would compromise him in his career, or, at least, get him horribly talked about, were they ever made sport of in the world. Where are his letters? Has Madame Sabaroff kept them? He longs to ask her, but he dare not.

He does not say to his cousin that he has more than once endeavoured to hint to Xenia Sabaroff that it would be sweet to him to recall the past, would she permit it. But he has elicited no response. She has evaded without directly avoiding him. She is no longer the impressionable, shy girl whom he knew in Russia, weighted with an unhappy fate, and rather alarmed by the very successes of her own beauty than flattered by them. She is a woman of the world, who knows her own value and her own power to charm, and has acquired the talent, which the world teaches, of reading the minds of others without revealing her own. *Saule pleureur!* the Petersburg Court ladies had used to call her in those early times when the tears had started to her eyes so quickly; but no one ever sees tears in her eyes now.

Gervase is profoundly troubled to find how much genuine emotion the presence of a woman, whose existence he had long forgotten, has power to excite in him. He does not like emotion of any kind; and in all his affairs of the heart he is accustomed to make others suffer, not himself. Vanity and wounded vanity enter so largely into the influences moulding human life, that it is very possible, if the sight of him had had power to disturb her, the renewal of association with her would have left him unmoved. But, as it is, he has been piqued, mortified, excited and attracted, and the admiration which Brandolin and Lawrence Hamilton and other men plainly show of her, is the sharpest spur to memory and to desire.

Whenever he has remembered Xenia Sabaroff, at such rare times as he has heard her name mentioned in the world, he has thought of her complacently, as dwelling in the solitudes of Baltic forests, entirely devoted to his memory. Women who are entirely devoted to their memory, men seldom trouble themselves to seek out; but to see her courted, sought and desired, more handsome than ever, and apparently wholly indifferent to himself, is a shock to his self-esteem, and galvanism to his dead wishes and slumbering recollections. He begins to perceive that he would have done better not to forget her quite so quickly.

Meanwhile, everybody staying at Surrenden, guided by a hint from Nina Curzon, begin to see a quantity of things which do not exist, and to exert their minds in endeavouring to remember a vast deal which they never heard with regard to both himself and her. No one knows anything, or has a shadow of fact to go on, but this is an insignificant detail which does not tie their tongues in the least. Nina Curzon has invention enough to supply any *lacunæ*, and in this instance her imagination is stimulated by a double jealousy; she is jealous of Lawrence Hamilton, whom she is inclined to dismiss, and she is jealous of Brandolin, whom she is inclined to appropriate.

Twenty-four hours have not elapsed

since the arrival of Gervase before she
has given a dozen people the intimate conviction that she knows all about him and
the Princess Sabaroff, and that there is
something very dreadful in it : much worse
than in the usual history of such relations.
Everything is possible in Russia, she says,
and has a way of saying this which
suggests unfathomable abysses of licence
and crime.

No one has the slightest idea what she
means, but no one will be behind any
other in conjecturing ; and there rises about
the unconscious figure of Xenia Sabaroff
a haze of vague, suggested, indistinct suspicion, like the smoke of the blue fires
which hide the form of the Evil One on
the stage in operas. Brandolin perceives
it, and is deeply irritated.

"What is it to me ?" he says to himself,
but says so in vain.

Fragments of these ingenious conjectures

and imaginary recollections come to his
ear and annoy him intensely; annoy him
the more because his swift intuitions and
unerring perceptions have told him from
his own observation that Xenia Sabaroff
does not see in Gervase altogether a
stranger, though she has greeted him as
such. Certain things are said which he
would like to resent, but he is powerless
to do so.

His days have been delightful to him
before the arrival of this other man at
Surrenden; now they are troubled and
embittered. Yet, he is not inclined to
break off his visit abruptly and go to
Scotland, Germany, or Norway, as might
be wisest. He is in love with Xenia
Sabaroff in a manner which surprises himself. He thought he had outlived that sort
of boyish and imaginative passion. But
she has a great power over his fancy and
his senses, and she is more like his earliest

met.

"Absurd that I should have an ideal at all at my age!" he thinks to himself, but as there are some who are never accompanied by that ethereal attendant, even in youth, so there are some whom it never leaves till they reach their graves.

Therefore, when he hears these vague, floating, disagreeable jests, he suffers acutely, and finds himself in the position which is, perhaps, most painful of all to any man who is a gentleman, that of being compelled to sit silent and hear a woman he longs to defend lightly spoken of, because he has no right to defend her, and would, indeed, only compromise her more if he attempted her defence.

But Dulcia Waverley is here, and her languid and touching ways, her delicate health and her soft sympathies, have an indescribable sorcery for him at all times, so that he thinks but very little, since her arrival, of anything else. Usk likes women who believe devoutly that he might have been a great politician if he had chosen, and who also believe in his ruined digestion. No one affects both these beliefs so intensely as Lady Waverley, and when she tells him that he could have solved the Irish Question in half-an-hour had he taken office, or that no one could understand his constitution except a German doctor in a bath in the Bœhmerwald, whither she goes herself every autumn, she does, altogether and absolutely, anything she chooses with him.

His wife sees that quite well, and dislikes it. but it might be so much worse, she reflects: it might be a woman out of society, or a public singer, or an American adventuress ; so she is reasonable and always makes *bonne mine* to Dulcia Waverley with her nerves, her cures. and her angelic smiles. After all, it does not make much matter, she thinks, if they like to go and drink nasty waters together, and poison themselves with sulphur, iron and potassium. It is one of the odd nineteenth-century ways of playing Antony and Cleopatra.

Notwithstanding the absorption of his thoughts. Usk, however, one day spares a moment from Lady Waverley and his own liver, to put together words dropped by different people then under his own roof; to ponder upon them ; and finally to interrogate his wife.

"Did you know that people say they

out preamble.

"Who?" asks the Lady of Surrenden, sharply.

"Madame Sabaroff and Gervase," he growls. "It'd be odd if they hadn't, as they've come to this house!"

"Of course, I knew they were friends, but there was never anything between them in the vulgar sense which you would imply renders them eligible for my society," replies Dorothy Usk, with the severity of a woman whose conscience is clear, and the tranquility of a woman who is telling a falsehood.

Usk stares at her.

"Well, if you knew it, you rode a dark horse, then, when you asked her here?"

who had had a certain sympathy for each other when honour kept them apart, there is nothing very culpable in it. What is your objection?"

"Oh, Lord! I've no objection; I don't care a straw," says her lord, with a very moody expression. "But Brandolin will, I suspect; she's certainly encouraged him. I think you might have shown us your cards."

"Lord Brandolin is certainly old enough to take care of himself in affairs of the heart, and experienced enough, too, if one is to believe all one hears," replies his wife. "What can he care, either, for a person he has known a few days? Whereas, the attachment of Gervase to her is of very long date and most romantic origin. He has loved her hopelessly for eight years."

Usk gives a grim guffaw.

"The constancy has had many interludes,

I suspect! Now I see why you took such a craze for the lady, but you might have said what you were after to me, at any rate. I could have hinted to Brandolin how the land lay, and he wouldn't have walked with his eyes shut into her net."

"Her 'net'? She is as cold as ice to him!" replies his wife, with disgust, "and were she otherwise, the loves of your friend are soon consoled. He writes a letter, takes a voyage, and throws his memories overboard. Alan's temperament is far more serious."

"If by serious you mean selfish, I agree with you. There isn't such another d—— egotist anywhere under the sun." And, much out of temper, Usk flings himself out of the room and goes to Lady Waverley, who is lying on a sofa in the small library. She has a headache, but her smile is sweet, her hand cool, her atmosphere soothing and delightful, with the blinds down and an odour of attar of roses.

If anyone were to tell Dolly Usk that she had been making up fibs on this occasion, she would be mortally offended and surprised. She would reply that she had only been *brodant un peu;* putting the thing as it ought to be put, as it must be put, if Gervase is to obtain the hand of Xenia Sabaroff, and if nobody is to know anything which ought not to be known. Indeed, she has pondered so much on this manner of putting it, that she has almost ended in believing that her version of the story is the true one.

"Brandolin's feelings, indeed!" she thinks, with great contempt. "As if any pain he might feel, if he did feel any, would not be due and fitting retribution upon him for the horrid life he has led, and the way he has played fast and loose with women. He can go back to his Hindoos, whose

friends."

Whereon, being in an irritated and unkind mood, she desires the servant, who just then announces the visit of the Rector of the parish, to show that reverend person into the small library, where she knows that Dulcia Waverley is trying to get rid of her headache. It is very seldom that she is unwise enough to indulge in this kind of domestic vengeance, but at this moment it seems sweet to her.

The unfortunate and innocent Rector finds the Lord of Surrenden monosyllabic and impolite, but Lady Waverley, woman-like, is wholly equal to the occasion, and in her sweet, low voice discourses of village choirs, and village readings, and village medicines and morals, with such divine patience and feminine adaptability, that the good man dismisses from his mind as im-

opened before him.

If ever there was purity incarnate, Dulcia Waverley looks it, with her white gown, her Madonna-like hair, her dewy, pensive eyes, and her appealing smile. She suggests the portraits in the Keepsakes and Forget-me-nots of fifty years ago; she has always about her the faint, old-fashioned perfume of attar of roses, and she wears her soft, fair hair in Raphaelite bands which, in any other woman, would look absurd; but her experience has told her that, despite all change in modes and manners, the surest weapons to subdue strong men, are still those old-fashioned charms of fragility and of apparent helplessness which made Othello weep when his bridal moon was young above the Venetian waters. Only if she had ever spoken candidly all she knows, which she never by any chance does, she would say that to succeed thus with Othello, or any other male creature, you must be, under all your apparent weakness, tenacious as a magnet and cold as steel. Therein lies the secret of all power ; the velvet glove and the iron hand may be an old saying, but it is a truth never old.

The conclusion which she has been compelled to draw from Gervase and his fragmentary story has seriously annoyed and shocked his cousin, but on reflection she decides to adhere to her invariable rule of ignoring all that is equivocal in it, and treating it accordingly.

No one has ever heard Lady Usk admit that there is the slightest impropriety in the relations of any of her guests : their unimpeachable immaculateness is one of those fictions, like the convenient fictions of the law, which are so useful that everyone agrees not to dispute their acceptance.

She will never know a person who is really compromised. Therefore, if there be any soil on the wings of her doves, she shuts her eyes to it so long as those of the world are shut. She has the agreeable power of never seeing but what she wishes to see; so, although for the moment she has been uncomfortably shocked, she recovers her composure rapidly, and persuades herself that Gervase merely spoke of a passing attachment, perfectly pure. Why should he not marry the object of it? To the mind of Dorothy Usk, that would make everything right. Things may have been wrong once, but that is nobody's business. Xenia Sabaroff is a charming and beautiful woman, and the silver mine beyond the Urals is a very real thing. Lady Usk is not a mercenary, she is even a generous, woman; but when English fortunes are so embarrassed, as they are in these days, with Socialists at the roots, and a Jacquérie tearing at the fruits of them, any solid fortune situated out of England would be of great use to any Englishman occupying a great position.

"We shall all of us have to live abroad before long," she reflects, with visions of Hodge chopping down her palms for fire-wood, and Sally smashing the porcelain in her model dairy.

No doubt the relations of her cousin and her guest have not been always what they ought to have been; but she does not wish to think of this, and she will not think of it; bygones are always best buried. The people who manage to be happy are those who understand the art of burying them, and use plenty of quicklime.

During the twenty years which have elapsed since her presentation, Dolly Usk has had a very varied experience of men and women, and has continually been solicited to interfere in their love affairs, or has even interfered without being solicited.   She likes the feeling of being a *diva ex machina* to her friends, and though she has so decidedly refused Gervase her assistance to discover the state of Xenia Sabaroff's feelings towards him, she begins in her own mind immediately to cast about for some indirect means of learning it, and arranges in her own fancy the whole story as it will sound prettiest and most proper if she be ever called on to relate it to the world.

She has a talent at putting such stories nicely in order, that anything which may be objectionable in them is altogether invisible, as a clever *faiseur* will so arrange old laces on a Court train that the darns and stains in them are wholly hidden away.   She likes exercising her ingenuity in this way, and although the narrative given her by Gervase has certainly seemed to her ob-jectionable, and one which places the hero of it in an unpleasant light, it may with tact be turned so as to show nothing but what is interesting. And to this end she also begins to drop little hints, little phrases, suggestive of that virtue of blameless and long constancy with which it is necessary to invest her cousin Alan, if he is to be made a centre of romance. She even essays these very delicately on the ear of Xenia Sabaroff, but they are met with so absolute a lack of response, so discouraging and cold, an absence of all understanding, that she cannot continue to try them in that direction.

"If that odious Brandolin were not here!" she thinks, irritably.

The attentions of Brandolin are very marked to the Princess Sabaroff, and are characterised by that carelessness of comment and that colour of romance which have always marked his interest in any woman. He is not a rival *à plaisanter*, she knows: but then she knows, too, that he never is serious in these matters.

When she first hears the story of Gervase, she heartily wishes that there were any pretence to get rid of Xenia Sabaroff, and hastily wonders what excuse she could make to break up her Surrenden circle. But, on reflection, she desires as strongly to retain her there; and as there is to be a child's costume ball on the occasion of the Babe's birthday a fortnight hence, she makes the children entreat their friend to stay for it, and adds her own solicitation to theirs. Madame Sabaroff hesitates, is inclined to refuse, but at length acquiesces.

Unfortunately, Usk, who always to his wife's mind represents the bull in the china shop with regard to any of her delicate and intricate combinations, insists that Brandolin shall not leave either. So the situation remains unchanged, though many guests come and go; some staying two days, some three or four.

Xenia Sabaroff has seen and suffered enough to make her not lightly won or easily impressed. She knows enough of the world to know her own value in it, and she has measured the brutality and the inconsistency which may lie under the most polished exterior.

"I am not old yet in years," she says once, "but I am very old in some things. I have no illusions."

"When there is a frost in spring the field flowers die," says Brandolin, softly, "but they come again."

"In the fields, perhaps," replies Xenia Sabaroff.

"And in the human heart," says Brandolin.

He longs to ask her what have been the relations between her and Gervase which people seem so sure have existed once; he longs to know whether it was the brutality of her husband, or the infidelity of any lover, which has taught her so early the instability of human happiness.

But he hesitates before any demand, however veiled or delicate, upon her confidence. He has known her such a little while, and he is conscious that she is not a *femme facile.* It is her greatest fascination for him. Though he is credited with holding women lightly, he is a man whose theories of what they ought to be are high and difficult to realise. Each day that he sees her at Surrenden tends to convince him more and more that she does realise them, despite the calumnies which are set floating round her name.

One day, amongst several new arrivals, a countryman of hers comes down from London, where, being momentarily Chargé d'Affairs of the Russian Legation, he has been cursing the heat, the dust, the deserted squares, the empty clubs, the ugly parks, and rushing out of town whenever he can for twenty-four hours, as he now comes to Surrenden from Saturday to Monday.

"*Comme un calicot! Comme un calicot!*" he says, piteously: "Such are the miseries of the diplomatic service."

He kisses the hands of Madame Sabaroff with ardour and reverence; he has known her in her own country. A gleam of amusement comes into his half-shut grey eyes as he recognises Gervase.

The next morning is Sunday; Usk and Dulcia Waverley are at church with the children and Lady Usk and Nina Curzon.

Brandolin strays into the small library, takes down a book and stretches himself on a couch. He half expects that Madame Sabaroff will come down before luncheon and also seek a book, as she did last Sunday. He lights a cigarette and waits, lazily watching the peacocks drawing their trains over the velvety turf without.   It is a lovely dewy morning, very fresh and fragrant after rains in the night.   He thinks he will persuade her to go for a walk ; there is a charming walk near, under deep trees, by a little brown brook full of forget-me-nots.

He hears a step, and looks up ; he does not see her, but the Russian Secretary, Gregor Litroff, always called " Toffy " by his female friends in England.

"*Dieu de Dieu !*   What an institution your English Sunday is !" says Litroff, with a yawn.   " I looked out of my window an hour ago, and beheld Usk in a tall hat, with his little boy on one side and my Lady Waverley on the other, solemnly going to church. How droll!   He would not do it in London."

" It is not more ridiculous to go to church in a tall hat than to prostrate your-self and kiss a wooden cross, as you would do if you were at home," says Brandolin,

irritation.

" That may be," says the Secretary, good-humouredly. "We do it from habit, to set an example, not to make a fuss. So, I suppose, does he."

" Precisely," says Brandolin, wondering how he shall get rid of this man.

" And he takes Lady Waverley for an example too ?" asks Litroff, with a laugh.

" Religion enjoins us," replies Brandolin, curtly, " to offer what we have most precious to the Lord."

The Secretary laughs again.

" That is very good," he says, with enjoyment.

Mr. Wootton comes in at that instant. He has been away, but has returned : the cooks at Surrenden are admirable. Brandolin sees his hopes of a *tête-à-tête* and a walk in the home wood fading farther and farther from view. Mr. Wootton has several telegram papers in his hand.

"All bad news, from all the departments," he remarks.

"There is nothing but bad news," says Brandolin. "It is painful to die by driblets. We shall all be glad when we have got the thing over; seen Windsor burnt, London sacked, Ireland admitted to the American Union, and Mr. and Mrs. Gladstone crowned at Westminster."

Mr. Wootton coughs; he does not like unseemly jests, nor to have the gravity and exclusiveness of the private intelligence he receives doubted. He turns to Litroff, talks of Russian politics, and brings the conversation round to the Princess Sabaroff.

Brandolin, appearing absorbed in his book, lies on his couch wondering whether he should meet her anywhere about the gardens if he went out. He listens angrily when he hears her name.

" Was she ever talked about?" asks Mr.
Wootton, searching the book-shelves.

" What charming woman is not?" returns
Litroff, gallantly.

" My dear Count," replies Mr. Wootton,
with grave rebuke, " we have thousands of
noble wives and mothers in England, before
whom Satan himself would be obliged to
bow in reverence."

" Ah, truly," says Litroff, "so have we,
I daresay; I have never asked."

"No doubt you have," says Mr. Wootton,
kindly. " The virtue of its women is the
great safeguard of a nation."

"One understands why England is losing
her nice equipose then, now," murmurs
Brandolin.

very natural——"

"What was natural?"

"That she should console herself."

"Ah! she did console herself?"

Litroff smiles. "Ask Lord Gervase, he was Lord Baird at that time. We all expected he would have married her when Sabaroff was shot."

"But it was Lustoff who shot Sabaroff in a duel about her?"

"Not about her. Lustoff quarrelled with him about a gambling affair, not about her at all, though people have said so. Lord Baird — Gervase — was, I am certain, her first lover, and has been her only one, as yet."

Brandolin flings his book with some violence on the floor, gets up and walks to the window. Mr. Wootton looks after him.

who is a good-natured man. " She was married when she was scarcely sixteen to a brute; she was immensely admired; she was alone in the midst of a society both loose and brilliant; Gervase laid siege to her *sans trêve*, and she was hardly more than a child then."

" Where there is no principle early mplanted——" begins Mr. Wootton.

But Litroff is not patient under preaching. " My dear sir," he says, impatiently, " principle (of that kind) is more easily implanted in plain women than in handsomer ones. Madame Sabaroff is a proud woman, which comes to nearly the same thing as a high-principled one. She has lived like a saint since Sabaroff was shot, and if she takes up matters with her early lover again, it will only be, I imagine, this time *pour le bon motif*. Anyhow, I don't see why we should blame her for the past, when the present shows us such an admirable and edifying spectacle as Miladi Waverley and Miladi Usk going to sit in church with George Usk between them."

Whereupon the Russian Secretary takes a *Figaro* off the newspaper table, and rudely opens it and flourishes between Mr. Wootton and himself, in sign that the conversation is ended.

Mr. Wootton has never been so treated in his life.

CHAPTER XI.

BRANDOLIN walks down the opening between
the glass doors into the garden. He paces
impatiently the green, shady walks where he
has seen her on other mornings than this.
It is lovely weather, and the innumerable
roses fill the warm, moist air with fragrance.
There is a sea breeze blowing from the sea
coast some thirteen miles away; his schooner
is in harbour there ; he thinks that it would
be wisest to go to it and sail away again
for as many thousand miles as he has just
left behind him. Xenia Sabaroff has a great
and growing influence over him, and he does
not wish her to exercise it and increase it if
this thing be true ; perhaps, after all, she

may be that kind of sorceress of which Mary Stuart is the eternal type, cold only that others may burn; *reculant pour mieux sauter*, exquisitely feminine, only to be more dangerously powerful. He does not wish to play the *rôle* of Chastelard, or of Douglas, or of Henry Darnley. He is stung to the quick by what he has heard said.

It is not new; since the arrival of Gervase the same thing has been hinted more or less clearly, more or less obscurely, within his hearing more than once; but the matter-of-fact words of Litroff have given the tale a kind of circumstantiality and substance which the vague uncertain suggestions of others did not do. Litroff has obviously no feeling against her; he even speaks of her with reluctance and admiration; therefore, his testimony has a truthfulness about it which would be lacking in any mere malicious scandal.

It is intensely painful to him to believe,

or even admit to himself as possible, that it may be thus true. She seems to him a very queen among women: all the romance of his temperament clothes her with idealic qualities. He walks on unconsciously till he has left the west garden and entered the wood which joins it, and the grassy seats made underneath the boughs. As he goes, his heart thrills, his pulse quickens: he sees Madame Sabaroff. She is seated on one of the turf banks reading; all the dogs of the house at her feet. He has almost walked on to her before he has perceived her.

"I beg your pardon," he murmurs, and pauses, undecided whether to go or stay.

She looks at him, a little surprised at the ceremony of his manner.

"For what do you beg my pardon? You are as free of the wood as I," she replies, with a smile. "I promised the children to keep their dogs quiet, and to

"You are too good to the children," says Brandolin, still with restraint. Her eyes open with increased surprise. She has never seen his manner, usually so easy, nonchalant, and unstudied, altered before.

"He must have heard bad news," she thinks, but says nothing and keeps her book open.

Brandolin stands near, silent and absorbed. He is musing what worlds he would give, if he had them, to know whether the story is true! He longs passionately to ask her in plain words, but it would be too brutal and too rude; he has not known her long enough to be able to presume to do so.

He watches the sunshine fall through the larch boughs on to her hands in their long, loose gloves, and touch the pearls which she always wears at her throat.

"How very much he is unlike himself!"

she thinks; she misses his spontaneous
and picturesque eloquence, his warm
abandon of manner, his caressing deference
of tone. At that moment there is a
gleam of white between the trees, a sound
of voices in the distance.

The family party are returning from
church, the dogs jump up and wag their
tails and bark their welcome, the Babe is
dashing on in advance. There is an end
of their brief *tête-a-tête;* he passionately
regrets the loss of it, though he is not
sure of what he would have said in
it.

"Always together!" says Dulcia Waver-
ley in a whisper to Usk, as she sees them.
"Does he know that he succeeds Lord
Gervase, do you think?"

"How should I know?" says Usk, "and
Dolly says there was nothing between her
and Gervase; nothing, at least it was all
in honour, as the French say."

"Oh, of course," agrees Lady Waverley, with her plaintive eyes gazing dreamily down the aisle of larch trees. The children have run on to Madame Sabaroff.

"Where is Alan?" thinks Dolly Usk, angrily, on seeing Brandolin.

Gervase, who is not an early riser, is then taking his coffee in bed as twelve strikes. He detests an English Sunday; although at Surrenden it is disguised as much as possible to look like any other day, still there is a Sunday feeling in the air, and Usk does not like people to play cards on Sunday; it is one of his ways of being virtuous vicariously.

"Primitive Christianity," says Brandolin, touching the white feathers of Dodo's hat and the white lace on her short skirts.

"We only go to sleep," replies the child, disconsolately. "We might just as well go to sleep at home, and it is so hot in that pew with all that red cloth!"

"My love!" says Dulcia Waverley, scandalised.

"Lady Waverley don't go to sleep!" cries the Babe in his terribly clear little voice. "She was writing in her hymn-book and showing it to papa."

No one appears to hear this indiscreet remark except Dodo, who laughs somewhat rudely.

"I was trying to remember the hymn of Faber's 'Longing for God,'" says Lady Waverley, who is never known to be at a loss. "The last verse escapes me. Can anyone recall it? It is so lamentable that Sectarianism prevents those hymns from being used in Protestant churches."

But no one there present is religious enough or poetic enough to help her to the missing lines.

"There is so little religious feeling anywhere in England," she remarks, with a sigh.

" It's the confounded levelling that destroys
it," says Usk, echoing the sigh.

"They speak of Faber," says Madame
Sabaroff. " The most beautiful and touching
of all his verses are those which express the
universal sorrow of the world."

And in her low, grave, melodious voice she
repeats a few of the lines of the poem :

The sea, unmated creature, tired and lone,
Makes on its desolate sands eternal moan.
Lakes on the calmest days are ever throbbing
Upon their pebbly shores with petulant sobbing.

The beasts of burden linger on their way
Like slaves, who will not speak when they obey ;
Their eyes, when their looks to us they raise,
With something of reproachful patience gaze.

Labour itself is but a sorrowful song,
The protest of the weak against the strong ;
Over rough waters, and in obstinate fields,
And from dark mines, the same sad sound it yields.

She is addressing Brandolin as she recites
them ; they are a little behind the others.

He does not reply, but looks at her with
an expression in his eyes which astonishes

and troubles her. He is thinking, as the music of her tones stirs his innermost soul, that he can believe no evil of her, will believe none. No, though the very angels of Heaven were to cry out against her.

"Where were you all this morning?" asks Lady Usk of her cousin, after luncheon.

"I never get up early," returns Gervase. "You know that."

"Brandolin was in the home wood with Madame Sabaroff as we returned from church," remarks Dolly Usk. "They were together under a larch tree. They looked as if they were on the brink of a quarrel, or at the end of one; either may be an interesting *rapprochement.*"

"I daresay they were only discussing some poet. They are always discussing some poet."

"Then they had fallen out over the poet. Poets are dangerous themes. Or perhaps she had been showing him your letters, if, as you seem to think, she carries them about with her everywhere like a reliquary."

"I never presumed to imagine that she had preserved them for a day."

"Oh! yes, you did. You had a vision of her weeping over them in secret every night, until you saw her here, and found her as unlike a *délaissée* as a woman can be."

"Certainly, she does not look that. Possibly, if Dido could have been dressed by Worth and Rodrigues, had diamonds as big as plovers' eggs, and been adored by Lord Brandolin, she would never have perished in despair. *Autres temps, autres mœurs.*"

He speaks with sullen and scornful bitterness; his handsome face is momentarily flushed.

Dorothy Usk looks at him with inquisitiveness; she has never known him fail to rely on his own attractions before.

"You are unusually modest," she replies.

"Certainly, in our days, if Æneas does not come back, we take somebody else ; sometimes we do that even if he does come back!"

Gervase is moodily silent.

"I never knew you 'funk a fence' before!" says his cousin to him, sarcastically.

"I have tried to say something to her," replies Gervase, moodily, "but she gives me no hearing, no occasion."

"I should have thought you were used well enough to make both for yourself," returns his cousin, with curt sympathy. "You have always been 'master of yourself, though women sigh,' a paraphrase of Pope at your service."

Gervase smiled, conscious of his past successes and willing to acknowledge them.

"But you see she does not sigh!" he murmurs, with a sense that the admission is not flattering to his own *amour propre.*

"You have lost the power to make her sigh, do you mean?"

"I make no impression on her at all. I am utterly unable to imagine her feelings, her sentiments—how much she would acknowledge, how much she would ignore."

"That is a confession of great helplessness! I should never have believed that you would be baffled by any woman, above all by a woman who once loved you."

"It is not easy to make a fire out of ashes."

"Not if the ashes are quite cold, certainly, but if a spark remains in them, the fire soon comes again."

He is silent; the apparent indifference of a person whom he believed to be living out her life in solitude, occupied only with his memory, annoys and mortifies him. He has never doubted his own power to write his name indelibly on the hearts of women.

"Perhaps she wishes to marry Brandolin?" suggests Dorothy Usk.

"Pshaw!" says Lord Gervase.

"Why pshaw?" repeats his cousin, persistently. "He would not be a man to my taste, and he hates marriage, and he has a set of Hindoos at St. Hubert's Lea, which would require as much cleansing as the Augean stable—but I daresay she doesn't know anything about them, and he may be persuading her that he thinks marriage opens the doors of Paradise—men can so easily pretend that sort of thing! A great many men have wanted to marry her, I believe, since she came back into the world after her seclusion. George declares that Brandolin is quite serious."

"Preposterous!" replies Lord Gervase.

"Really, I don't see that," replies his judicious cousin. "A great many women have wanted to marry *him*, though one wonders why. Indeed, I have heard some of them declare that he is wholly irresistible when he chooses."

"With Hindoos, perhaps," says Gervase.

"With our women," says his cousin. "Lady Mary Jardine died of a broken heart because he wouldn't look at her."

"Pray spare me the roll-call of his victims," says Lord Gervase, irritably; he is passionately jealous of Brandolin. He himself had forgotten Xenia Sabaroff, and forgotten all his obligations to her, when she had been, as he always had believed, within reach of his hand if he stretched it out; but viewed as a woman whom other men wooed and another man might win, she has become to him intensely to be desired and to be disputed. He has been a spoiled child of fortune and of the drawing-rooms all his years, and the slightest opposition is intolerable to him.

"I have no doubt," continues Dorothy Usk, "that if he were aware you had a prior claim, if he thought or knew that you had ever enjoyed her sympathy, he would immediately withdraw and leave the field; he is a very proud man, with all his carelessness, and would not, I think, care to be second to anybody in the affections of a woman whom he seriously sought."

"What do you mean?" asks Gervase, abruptly, pausing in his walk to and from the boudoir.

"Only what I say," she answers. "If you wish to *éloigner* Brandolin, give him some idea of the truth.

Gervase laughs a little.

"On my honour," he thinks, with some bitterness, "for sheer uncompromising meanness, there is nothing comparable to the suggestions which a woman will make to you!"

"I couldn't do that," he says aloud, "what would he think of me?"

"My dear Alan," replies Dorothy Usk, impatiently, "when a man has behaved to any woman as you, by your own account, have behaved to Madame Sabaroff, I think it is a little late in the day to pretend to much elevation of feeling."

" You do not understand——"

" I have always found," says his cousin, impatiently " that whenever we presume to pronounce an opinion on any man's conduct and think ill of it, we are always told that we don't understand anything. When we flatter the man, or compliment him on his conduct, there is no end to the marvellous powers of our penetration, the fineness of our instincts, the accuracy of our intuitions!"

Gervase does not hear, his thoughts are elsewhere; he is thinking of Xenia Sabaroff as he saw her first in the Salle des

her friends; but that time is long ago, very long, as the life of women counts, and Xenia Sabaroff is now perfect mistress of her own emotions, if emotions she ever feels. Gervase cannot for one moment tell whether the past is tenderly remembered by her, is utterly forgotten, or is only recalled to be touched and dismissed without regret. He is a vain man but vanity has no power to reassure him here.

In the warm afternoon of the next day the children are in the school-room, supposed to be preparing their lessons for the morrow; but the German governess, who is alone as guardian of order in the temple of intellect, has fallen asleep, with flies buzzing about her blonde hair, and her blue spectacles pushed up on her forehead, and Dodo has taken advantage of the fact to go and lean out of one of the windows, whilst her sister draws a caricature of the sleeping virgin from Deutschland, and the Babe slips away from his books to a mechanical Punch, which, contraband in the school-room, is far dearer to him than his Gradus and the Rule of Three.

Dodo, with her hands thrust amongst her abundant locks, lolls with half her body in the air, and, by twisting her neck almost to dislocation, manages to see round an ivy-grown buttress of the east wall, and to espy people who are getting on their horses at the south doors of the building.

"They are going out riding and I am shut up here!" she groans. "Oh, what a while it takes one to grow up!"

"Who are going to ride?" asks Lillie, too fascinated by her drawing to leave it.

"Lots of them," replies Dodo, who speaks four languages, and her own worst of all. "All of them, pretty nearly. Mamma's on

Pepper, and Lady Waverley's got Bo-peep
—she's always nervous you know. I can't
see very much 'cause of the ivy. Oh,
there's the Princess on Satan, nobody else
could ride Satan ; Lord Brandolin's put her
up, and now he's riding by her—they're
gone now—and papa's stopping behind them
all to do something to Bo-peep's girths"—
whereat the dutiful Dodo laughs rudely,
as she laughed coming home from church.

The sound of the horses' hoofs going
further away down the avenue comes
through the stillness, as her voice and
her laughter cease.

"What a shame to be shut up here
just because one isn't old," she groans, as
she listens enviously. The sun is pouring
liquid gold through the ivy leaves, the air
is hot and fragrant, gardeners are watering
the flower-beds below, and the sweet, moist
scent comes up to Dodo's nostrils and makes
her writhe with longing to get out ; not that

she is by any means ardently devoted to nature, but she loves life, movement, gaiety, and she dearly loves showing off her figure on her ponies, and being flirted with by her father's friend.

"I am sure Lord Brandolin is in love with her, awfully in love," she says, as she peers into the distance where the black form of Satan is just visible through far-off oak boughs.

"With whom?" asks Lillie, getting up from her caricature to lean also out over the ivy.

"Xenia," says Dodo. She is very proud of calling her friend Xenia. "Take care Goggles don't wake, or she'll see what you've been doing."

The lady from Deutschland is always known to them by this endearing epithet.

"I don't care," says Lillie, kicking her bronze boots in the air. "Do you think she'll marry Lord Brandolin?"

"Who? Goggles?"

"The idea!" They laugh deliciously.

"You say he's in love with Xenia. If they're in love they will marry," says Lillie, pensively.

"No, they won't ; people who are in love never marry," replies Dodo.

"What do they do then?" inquires the younger sister.

"They marry somebody else, and ask the one they like to go and stay with them. It is much better," she adds. "It is what I shall do."

"Why is it better? It's a roundabout way," objects Lillie. "I shouldn't care to marry at all," she adds, "only one can't ever be Mistress of the Robes if one

the French governess, entering at that moment. "*Ou donc mettez vous l'amour?*"

"*Nous ne sommes pas des bourgeoises,*" returns' Dodo, very haughtily.

The Babe, sitting astride on a chair, trying to mend his mechanical Punch, who screamed and beat his wife *absolument comme la nature*, as the French governess said, before he was broken, hears the discourse of his sisters and muses on it. He is very fond of Brandolin and he adores his Princess: he would like them to live together, and he would go and see them without his sisters, who tease him, and without Boom, who lords it over him. Into his busy and precocious little brain there enters the resolution to *pousser la machine*, as his governess would call it.

The Babe has a vast idea of his own resources in the way of speech and invention, and he has his mother's tendencies to interfere with other people's affairs, and is quite of an opinion that if he had the management of most things he should better them. He has broken his Parisian Punch in his endeavour to make it say more words than it could say, but this slight accident does not affect his own admiration and belief in his own powers, any more than to have brought a great and prosperous empire within measureable distance of civil war affects a statesman's conviction that he is the only person who can rule that empire. The Babe, like Mr. Gladstone, is, in his own eyes, infallible. Like the astute diplomatist he is, he waits for a good opportunity; he is always where the ladies are, and his sharp little wits have been preternaturally quickened in that atmosphere of what the French call "*l'odeur feminin*."

He has to wait some days for his occasion; the frank and friendly intercourse which existed at first between Brandolin and Madame Sabaroff is altered; they are never alone, and the pleasant discussions on poets and poetry, on philosophers and follies, in the gardens in the forenoon are discontinued ; neither could very well say why, but the presence of Gervase chills and oppresses both of them and keeps them apart. She has the burden of memory, he the burden of suspicion ; and suspicion is a thing so hateful and intolerable to the nature of Brandolin that it makes him miserable to feel himself guilty of it.

But, one morning, the Babe coaxes her out to go with him to his garden ; a floral republic, where a cabbage comes up cheek by jowl with a gloxiana, and plants are plucked up by the roots to see if they are growing aright. The Babe's system of horticulture is to dig intently for ten minutes in all directions, to make himself very red in the face, and then to call Dick, Tom, or Harry, any under-gardeners who may be near, and say : "Here, do it, will you?"

Nevertheless, he retains the belief that he is the creator and cultivator of this his garden, as M. Grevy believes that he is the chief person in the French Republic: and he takes Madame Sabaroff to admire it.

" It would look better if it were a little more in order," she permits herself to observe.

" Oh, that's their fault," says the Babe, just as M. Grevy would say of disorder in the Chambers, the Babe meaning Dick, Tom, or Harry, as the President would mean Clemenceau, Rochefort, or M. de Mun.

" My dear Babe, how exactly you are like the Head of a Department," says Brandolin, who has followed them out of the house and comes up behind them. " According to the Head of a Department, it is never the head that is at fault, always the under-strappers. May I inquire since when it has become the fashion to set sunflowers with their heads downwards ?"

"I wanted to see if the roots would turn after the sun," says the Babe, and regards his explanation as triumphant.

"And they only die! How perverse of them. You would become a second Newton, if your destiny were not already cast, to dazzle the world by a blending of Beau Brummel and Sir Joseph Paxton."

The Babe looks a little cross: he does not like to be laughed at before his Princess. He has got his opportunity, but it vexes him; he has an impression that his companions will soon drift into forgetting both him and his garden. Since the approach of Brandolin the latter has said nothing.

The children's gardens are in a rather wild and distant part of the grounds of Surrenden. It is noon: most people staying in the house are still in their own rooms; it is solitary, sunny, still; a thrush is singing in a jessamine thicket, there is no other sound except that of a gardener's

laurel hedge.

The Babe feels that it is now or never for his *coup de maitre*.

He plucks a rose, the best one he has, and offers it to Madame Sabaroff, who accepts it gratefully, though it is considerably earwig-eaten, and puts it in her corsage.

The eyes of Brandolin follow it wistfully.

The child glances at them alternately from under his hair, then his small features assume an expression of cherubic innocence and unconsciousness. The most rusé little rogue in the whole kingdom, he knows how to make himself look like a perfect reproduction of Sir Joshua Reynolds' Artlessness or Infancy. He gazes up in Xenia Sabaroff's face, with angelic simplicity admirably assumed.

"When you marry him," he says, pointing to Brandolin with admirably affected naïveté, "you will let me hold up your train, won't you? I always hold up my friends' trains when they marry. I have a page's dress, Louis something or other, and a sword, and a velvet cap with a badge and a feather; I always look very well."

"Oh, what an odious *petit maitre* you will be when you are a man, my dear Babe!" says Xenia Sabaroff.

She does not take any notice of his opening words, but a flush of colour comes over her face and passes as quickly as it came.

"*Petit maitre!* what is that?" says the Babe. "But you will let me, won't you? And don't marry him till the autumn, or even the winter, because the velvet makes me so hot when the day is hot, and the dress wouldn't look nice made in thin things."

"Could I only add my prayer to his,"

murmurs Brandolin, "and hope that in the autumn——"

Xenia Sabaroff looks at him with a strange gaze; it is penetrating, dreamy, wistful, inquiring.

"We jest as the child jests," she says, abruptly, and walks onward.

"I do not jest," says Brandolin.

The Babe glances at them under his thick eyelashes, and being a *fine mouche*, only innocent in appearance, he runs off after a butterfly. He has not been brought up in a feminine atmosphere of *poudre de riz* and *lait d'iris* without learning discretion.

CHAPTER XII.

"THE Babe is a better courtier than gardener," says Xenia Sabaroff, as she shakes a green aphid out of her rose: her tone is careless, but her voice is not quite under her command and has a little tremor in it.

Brandolin looks at her with impassioned eyes: he has grown very pale.

"It is no jest with me," he says, under his breath. "I would give you my life if you would take it?"

The last words have the accent of an interrogation, of an appeal.

"That is to say a great deal," replies Xenia Sabaroff: she is startled, astonished, troubled; she was not expecting any such entire avowals.

"Many men must have said as much to you who have more to recommend them than I. Say something to me: what will you say?"

She does not immediately reply; she looks on the ground, and absently traces patterns on the path with the end of her long walking-stick.

"Do you know," she says at last, after a silence which seems to him endless, "do you know that there are people who believe that I have been the *délaissée* of Lord Gervase. They do not phrase it so roughly, but that is what they say."

Brandolin's very lips were white, but his voice does not falter for one moment, as he answered: "They will not say it in my hearing."

"And knowing that they say it, you would still offer me your name?"

"I do so."

"And you would ask me nothing save what I choose to tell you?"

The sunny air seems to turn round with him for an instant; his brain grows dizzy; his heart contracts with a sickening pain; but in the next moment a great wave of strong and perfect faith in the woman he cares for lifts his soul up on it it as a sea wave lifts a drowning man to land.

"You shall tell me nothing save what you choose," he says, clearly and very tenderly. "I have perfect faith in you. Had I less than that, I would not ask you to be my wife."

She looks at him with astonishment and with wondering admiration.

"Yet you know so little of me!" she murmurs, in amaze.

"I love you," says Brandolin; then he kisses her hand with great reverence.

The tears which she had thought driven from her eyes for ever, rise in them now.

"You are very noble," she replies, and leaves her hand for an instant within his.

The Babe, who has been watching from behind a tuft of laurel, can control his impatience no longer, but comes out of his ambush and runs towards them, regardless of how undesired he may be.

"Dodo says that women never marry anybody they love," he says, breathlessly, "but that is not true, is it, and you will let me carry your train?"

"Hush, my dear," says Xenia Sabaroff, laying her hand on the child's shoulder, while there is a sound in her voice which subdues to silence even the audacious spirit of the Babe.

"Give me time to think," she says, in a low tone to Brandolin, and then, with her hand still on the little boy's shoulder, she turns away from him and walks slowly towards the house.

The child walks silently and shyly beside her, his happy vanity troubled for once by the sense that he has made some mistake and that there are some few things still in the universe which he does not quite entirely understand.

"You are not angry?" he asks her at last, with a vague terror in his gay and impudent little soul.

"Angry with you?" says Xenia Sabaroff. "My dear child, no. I am, perhaps, angry with myself—myself of many years ago."

The Babe is silent: he does not venture to ask any more, and he has a humiliating feeling that he is not first in the thoughts of Madame Sabaroff; nay, that though his rose is in her gown and her hand upon his shoulder, she has almost, very nearly almost, forgotten him.

Brandolin does not attempt to follow her. Her great charm for him consists in the power she possesses of compelling him to control his impulses. He walks away by himself through the green shadows of the boughs, wishing for no companionship save hers. He is fully aware that he has done a rash, perhaps an utterly unwise, thing in putting his future into the hands of a woman of whom he knows so little, and has perhaps the right to suspect so much. Yet he does not repent.

He does not see her again before dinner. She does not come into the library at the tea hour; there is a large dinner that night; county people are there as well as the house party. He has to take in a stupid woman, wife of the Lord Lieutenant, who thinks him the most absent-minded and unpleasant person she has ever known, and wonders how he has got his reputation as a wit. He is so seated that he cannot even see Xenia Sabaroff, and he chafes and frets throughout the dinner, from the bisque soup to the caviare biscuit, and thinks what an idiotic thing the habits of society have made of human life.

When he is fairly, at rare intervals, goaded

into speech, he utters paradoxes, and suggests views so startling, that the wife of the Lord Lieutenant is scandalised, and thinks the lunacy laws are defective if they cannot include and incarcerate him. She feels sure that the rumour about the Hindoo women at St. Hubert's Lea is entirely true.

After dinner, he is free to approach the lady of his thoughts, but he endeavours in vain to tell from her face what answer he will receive, what time and meditation may have done or undone for him. She avoids the interrogation of his eyes, and is surrounded by other men as usual.

The evening seems to him intolerably long and intolerably tedious. It is, however, for others very gay. There is an improvised dance, ending in an impromptu cotillon, and following on an act of a comic opera given with admirable spirit by Lady Dawlish, Mrs. Curzon, and some of the younger men. Everyone is amused, but the hours seemed very slow to him : Gervase scarcely leaves her side at all, and Brandolin, with all his chivalrous refusal and unchanging resolution to allow no shadow of doubt to steal over him, feels the odious whispers he has heard, and the outspoken words of Litroff recur to his memory and weigh on him like the incubus of a nightmare. With a sensation of dread he realises that it is possible, do what he may, that they may haunt him so all his life. A man may be always master of his acts, but scarcely always of his thoughts.

"But I will never ask her one syllable," he thinks, "and I will marry her to-morrow if she chooses."

But will she choose?

He is far from sure. He pleases her intelligence : he possesses her friendship ; but whether he has the slightest power to touch her heart, he does not know. If he loved her less than he does he would be more confident. As the interminable hours wear away, and the noise and absurdities of the cotillon are at their height, she, who never dances anywhere, drops her fan, and he is before the others in restoring it to her. As she takes it, she says in a low voice: "Be in the small library at eleven to-morrow."

"Why will you always treat me as a stranger, Madame Sabaroff?" murmurs Gervase to her that same night when, for a moment, he is alone near her, while the cotillon draws to a close.

"You are a stranger—to me," replies Xenia Sabaroff; and as she speaks she looks full at him.

He colours with discomfiture.

"Because, in the due course of nature, I have succeeded to my father's title, you seem to consider that I have changed my whole identity," he says, with great irritation.

white ostrich feathers of her fan. He is vaguely encouraged by that silence.

"Strangers!" he says, with annoyance and reproach, "that is surely a very cold and cruel word between those who once were friends?"

The direct appeal to her makes her look up once more with greater hauteur in the coldness of her face.

"Sir, I think when people have forgotten that each other exist, it is as though they had never met. They are, perhaps, something more distant still than strangers, for, to strangers, friendship in the future is possible; but those who have been separated by oblivion on the one hand, and by contempt on the other, are parted as surely and eternally as though death had divided them."

Gervase gathers some solace from the very strength of the words. She would not, he thinks, feel so strongly unless she felt more than he allows; he gazes at her with feigned humility and unfeigned admiration and regret.

"If Madame Sabaroff," he murmurs, "can doubt her own powers of compelling remembrance, she is the one person only on earth who can do so."

She is stung to anger?

"I am really at a loss to decide whether you are intentionally insolent or unintentionally insincere. You are possibly both."

"I am neither! I am only a man who passionately and uselessly rebels against his fate."

"Who regrets his own actions, you mean to say. That is nothing uncommon."

"Well, who regrets the past, if you will put it so, and who would atone for it would you allow him."

"Atone! Do you suppose that you owe me reparation? It is I who owe you thanks for a momentary oblivion which did me immeasurable service."

"That is a very harsh doctrine. The Princess Xenia, whom I knew, was neither so stern nor so sceptical."

"The Princess Xenia, whom you knew, was a child, a foolish child; she is dead, quite as much dead as though she were under solid square feet of Baltic ice. Put her from your thoughts; you will never awake her."

Then she rises and leaves him and goes out of the ballroom.

Soon after she leaves the ballroom altogether, and goes to her bedchamber.

Brandolin goes to his before the cotillon is over, but he sleeps very little. He longs for the morrow, and yet he dreads it. "*Quand même*," he murmurs, as from his bed he sees the white dawn over the dark masses of the Surrenden woods. Tell him what she may, he thinks, he will give her his life if she will take it. He is madly in love, no doubt ; but there is something nobler and purer than the madness of love, than the mere violent instincts of passion, in his loyalty to her. Before anything he cherishes the honour of his name and race, and he is willing, blind-fold, to trust her with it.

That morning it seems to him as if the hours would never pass, though they are few, until the clock strikes eleven. The house is still, almost everyone is asleep, for the cotillon, successful as only unpremeditated things ever are, had lasted till the sun was high, and the dew on the grass of the garden was dry.

With a thickly beating heart, nervous and eager, as though he were a boy of sixteen seeking his first love-tryst, he enters the small library far before the hour, and waits for her there, pacing to and fro the floor. The room is full of memories of her ; here they have talked

on rainy days and have strolled out on
to the lawns on fine ones; there is the
chair which she likes best, and there the
volume she had taken down yesterday;
could it be only ten days since standing
here he had seen her first in the distance
with the children? Only ten days! It
seems to him ten years, ten centuries.

The morning is very still, a fine, soft
rain is falling, wet jessamine flowers tap
the panes of the closed windows, a great
apprehension seems to make his very
heart stand still.

As the clock points to the hour she
enters the room.

She is very pale, and wears a morning
gown of white plush, which trails behind her
in a silver shadow. He kisses her hands
passionately, but she draws them away.

"Wait a little," she says, gently. "Wait
till you know—whatever there is to know."

"I want to know but one thing."

She smiled a little sadly.

"Oh! you think so now, because you are in love with me. But in time to come, when that is passed, you will not be so easily content. If "—she hesitates a moment—"if there is to be any community between our lives you must be quite satisfied as to my past. It is your right to be so satisfied, and were you not so, some time or other we should both be wretched."

His eyes flash with joy.

"Then"—he begins, breathlessly.

"Oh! how like a man that is!" she says, sadly. "To think but of the one thing, of the one present moment, and to be ready to give all the future in pawn for it! Wait to hear everything. And first of all I must tell you that Lord Gervase also wrote me a letter this morning in which he asks me to marry him."

"And you?"

"I shall not marry Lord Gervase. But I will not disguise from you that once I would have done so gladly had I been free to do it."

Brandolin is silent: he changes colour.

"I bade him come here for my answer," she continues. "He will be here in a few minutes. I wish you to remain in the large library so that you may hear all that I say to him."

"I cannot do that, I cannot play the part of eavesdropper."

"You will play that part, or any other that I ask you, if you love me," she says, with a touch of imperiousness.

"Do you not see," she goes on, with more gentleness, "that if our lives are to be passed near one another—I do not say that they are, but you seem to wish it— you must first of all be convinced of the truth of all I tell you. If one doubt, one suspicion remain, you will in time become unable to banish it. It would grow and grow until you were mastered by it. You believe in what I tell you now, but how long would you believe after marriage ?"

"I want no proof, I only want your word. Nay, I do not even want that. I will ask you nothing. I swear that I will never ask you anything."

"That is very beautiful; and I am sure that you mean it now. But it could not last. You are a very proud man; you are *gentilhomme de race*. It would in time become intolerable to you if you believed that any one living man had any title to point a finger of scorn at you. You have a right to know what my relations were with Lord Gervase; it is necessary for all the peace of our future that you should know everything; know that there is nothing more left for you to know. You can only be convinced of that if you yourself hear what I say to him. Go; and wait there!"

Brandolin hesitates. To listen unseen is a part which seems very cowardly to him, and yet she is right, no doubt; all the peace of the future may depend on it. He is ready to pledge himself blindly in the dark in all ways, but he knows that she, in forbidding him to do so, speaks the word of wisdom, of foresight, and of truth.

"Go!" she repeats. "Men have a thousand ways of proving the truth of whatever they say; we have none, or next to none. If you refuse me this, the sole poor evidence that I can produce, I will never be to you anything that you now wish; never, that I swear to you."

He hesitates, and looks at her with a long inquiring regard. Then he bows and goes.

After all, she is within her rights. She has no other means to show him with any proof what this man, whose name is so odiously entangled with her own, has, or has not, been to her.

The house is still quite silent, and no one is likely to come into those rooms until much later. Every syllable said in the small library can be heard in any part of the larger one. He stands in the embrasure of one of the windows, the velvet curtains making a screen behind him. He seems to wait for hours ; in reality only five minutes have passed when he hears the door of the great library open, and Gervase passes quickly through the apartment without seeing him, and goes on into the one where she awaits his coming.

"Are you really risen so early ?" she says, with a sarcastic coldness in her voice. "I remembered afterwards that it was too cruel to name to you any hour before noon."

"You are unkind," he answers. "To hear what I hope to hear, you may be sure that I would have gone through much greater trials than even rising with the lark, had you commanded it."

His words are light, but his accent is tender and appealing.

"What do you hope to hear?" she asks, abruptly. The question embarrasses him and sounds cold.

"I hope to hear that you pardon me the past and will deign to crown my future."

"I pardon you the past, certainly. With neither your present nor your future have I anything to do."

"You say that very cruelly; so cruelly that it makes your forgiveness more unkind than your hatred would be."

"I intend no unkindness. I merely wish to express indifference. Perhaps I am even mistaken in saying that I entirely forgive you. When I remember that you once possessed any influence over me, I scarcely do forgive you, for I am forced to despise myself."

"Those are very hard words! Perhaps in the past I was unworthy of having known and loved you; but if you will believe in my regret, and allow me occasion to atone, you shall never repent of your indulgence. Pray hear me out, Xenia——"

"You cannot call me by that name. It is for my friends; you are not numbered amongst them."

"I would be much more than your friend, if you will be my wife."

"It is too late," she replies, and her voice is as cold as ice.

"Why too late? We have all the best of our lives unspent before us."

"When I say too late, I mean that if you had said as much to me after the death of Prince Sabaroff, I should have accepted your hand, and I should have spent the whole remainder of my existence in repenting that I had done so; for I should soon have fathomed the shallowness of your character,

and you."

"You are not merciful, Madame!"

He is bitterly humbled and passionately incensed.

"Were you merciful?" she asks him, with the sound of a great anger, carefully controlled, vibrating in her voice. "I was a child, taken out of a country convent, and married as ignorantly as a bird is trapped. I had rank, and I was burdened by it. I was in a great world, a great Court, and I was terrified by them. The man I had been given to was a gambler, a drunkard and a brute. He treated me in private as he had treated the women captured in Turkestan, or sold as slaves in Persia. You knew that; you were his intimate associate. You used your opportunities to interest me and win your way into my confidence. I had no one in the whole world that I could trust. I did trust you."

She pauses a moment.

Gervase does not dare reply.

" You were so gentle, so considerate, so full of sympathy; I thought you a very angel. A girl of sixteen or seventeen sees the face of St. John in the first Faust who finds his way into her shut soul! You made me care for you; I do not deny it! But why did I care? Because I saw in you the image of a thousand things you were not. Because I imagined that my own fanciful ideal existed in you, and you had the ability to foster the illusion."

"But why recall all this?" he says, entreatingly. "Perhaps I was unworthy of your innocent attachment, of your exalted imaginations. I dare not say that I was not; but now that I meet you again, now that I care for you ten thousand—ten million times more——"

"What is that to me?" she says, with almost insolent coldness. "It was not I who loved you—but a child who knew no better, and whose heart was so bleeding from the tortures of another man, that the first hand which soothed it could take it as one takes a wounded bird! But when my eyes opened to your drift and your desires, when I saw that you were no better than other men, that you tried to tempt me to the lowest forms of intrigue under cover of your friendship with my husband, then, child though I was, I saw you as you were, and I hid myself from you! You thought that Sabaroff exiled me from his jealousy of you to the northern estates, but it is not so. I entreated him to let me leave Petersburg, and he had grown tired of torturing me and let me go!"

"You blame me for being merely human. I loved you not better but not worse than men do love."

"I blame you for having been insincere, treacherous, dishonest. You approached me under cover of the most delicate and forbearing sympathy and reverence, and you only wore those masks to cover the vulgar designs of a most commonplace Lothario. Of course, now I know that one must not play with fire unless one is willing to be burned. I did not know it then. I was a stupid, unhappy, trembling child, full of poetic fancies, and alone in a dissolute crowd. When you could not make me what you wished to make me, I seemed very tame and useless to you. You turned to more facile women, no doubt, and you left Russia."

"I left Russia under orders, and I wrote to you. I wrote to you repeatedly; you never answered."

"No; I had no wish to answer you. I had seen you as you were, and the veil had fallen from my eyes. I burnt your letters as they came to me. But after the death of Prince Sabaroff you were careful to write no more!"

Gervase colours hotly; there is an accent in the words which makes them strike him like whips.

"If you had written to me after that," she continues, "perhaps I should have answered you, perhaps not: I cannot tell. When you knew that I was set free, you were silent; you stayed away, I know not where. I never saw you again; I never heard from you again. Now, I thank you for your neglect and oblivion, but at the same time, I confess that it made me suffer. I was very young still and romantic. For a while I expected every month which melted the snow would bring you back. So much I admit, though it will flatter you."

It does not flatter him as she says it; rather it wounds him. He has a hateful sense of his own impotency to stir her one hand's breadth, to breathe one spark of

ever.

"I do not think," she continues, "that I ever loved you in the sense that women can love; but you had the power to make me suffer, to feel your oblivion, to remember you when you had forgotten me. When I went into the world again I heard of your successes with others, and gradually I came to see you in your true light, and, almost the drunken brutality of Prince Sabaroff seemed to me a manlier thing than your half-hearted and shallow erotics had been. Now, when we meet again by pure hazard in the same country house, you do me the honour to offer me your hand after eight years. I can only say, as I have said before, that it is seven years too late!"

"Too late, only because Lord Brandolin now is everything to you."

"Lord Brandolin may possibly be something to me in the future. But, if Lord

Pale and agitated as no other woman had ever seen him, Gervase bows low and leaves her abruptly, pushing open one of the glass doors on to the garden and closing it with a clash behind him.

Xenia Sabaroff goes towards the large library, her silvery train catching the lights and shadows as she goes.

Brandolin meets her with his hands out-stretched.

" You are content, then?" she asks.

" I am more than content—if I may be allowed to atone to you for all that you have suffered."

His own eyes are dim as he speaks.

" But you know that the world will always say that he was my lover?"

with deep emotion.

Brandolin smiles.

"Oh! I cannot claim so much as that, but certainly I have a great love."

.   .   .   .

"I'm awfully glad that prig's got spun," says George Usk, as Gervase receives a telegram from the Foreign Office, which requires his departure from Surrenden at four o'clock that afternoon.

"Spun! What imagination!" says his wife, very angrily. "Who should have spun him, pray, will you tell me?"

"We shall never hear it in so many words," says Usk, with a grim complacency, "but I'll swear, if I die for it, that he's asked your Russian friend to marry him and that she's said she won't. Very wise of her too, especially if, as you imply, they carried on together years ago ; he'd be eternally throwing the past in her teeth ; he's what the Yanks call a 'tarnation mean cuss.'"

" I never implied anything of the sort," answers the Lady of Surrenden, with great decorum and dignity. " I never suppose that all my friends are not all they ought to be, whatever *yours* may leave to be desired. If he were attached long ago to Madame Sabaroff, it is neither your affair nor mine. It may possibly concern Lord Brandolin if he has the intentions which you attribute to him."

" Brandolin can take care of himself," says Usk, carelessly. " He knows the time of day as well as anybody, and I don't know why you should be rough on it, my lady : it will be positively refreshing if anybody marries after one of your house parties ; they generally only get divorced after them !"

" The Waverleys are very good friends still, I believe," says Dorothy Usk, coldly.

The reply seems irrelevant, but to the ear of George Usk it carries considerable relevancy.

He laughs, a little nervously.

" Oh, yes: so are we, aren't we?"

" Certainly," says the mistress of Surrenden.

.   .   .   .

At the first Drawing-room this year, the admired of all eyes, and the centre of all comment, is the Lady Brandolin.

THE END.

PRINTED BY
TILLOTSON AND SON, MAWDSLEY STREET
BOLTON

HURST & BLACKETT'S

LIST OF NEW WORKS.

LONDON:

13, GREAT MARLBOROUGH STREET, W.

MESSRS. HURST AND BLACKETT'S
LIST OF NEW WORKS.

REMINISCENCES OF THE COURT AND TIMES OF KING ERNEST OF HANOVER. By the Rev. C. A. WILKINSON, M.A., His Majesty's Resident Domestic Chaplain. 2 vols. With portrait of the King. 21s.

"An interesting book, entitled 'Reminiscences of the Court and Times of King Ernest of Hanover,' has just been published by Messrs. Hurst and Blackett. The two volumes in which these reminiscences of a septuagenarian are comprised abound in characteristic stories of the old king, in anecdotes of many celebrities English and foreign, of the early part of this century, and, indeed, of all kinds and conditions of men and women with whom the author was brought in contact by his courtly or pastorial office."—*St. James's Gazette.*

"One of the most interesting and amusing books of this season; it abounds in good and new stories of King Ernest, and also of a perfect host of celebrities, both English and German."—*Truth.*

THE EGYPTIAN CAMPAIGNS, 1882 TO 1885, AND THE EVENTS WHICH LED TO THEM. By CHARLES ROYLE, Barrister-at-Law, of ALEXANDRIA. 2 vols. demy 8vo. Illustrated by Maps and Plans. 30s.

"Mr. Royle has done well in the interests of historical completeness to describe not only the entire military drama, but also the political events connected with it, and whoever reads the book with care has gone a considerable way towards mastering the difficult Egyptian question."—*Athenæum.*

"The Egyptian fiasco has found in Mr. Royle a most painstaking, accurate, and judicious historian. From a literary point of view his volumes may be thought to contain too many unimportant incidents, yet their presence was necessary perhaps, in a complete record, and the most fastidious reader will unhesitatingly acquit Mr. Royle of filling his pages with anything that can be called padding."—*St. James's Gazette.*

THE PALACE AND THE HOSPITAL; or, CHRONICLES OF GREENWICH. By the REV. A. G. L'ESTRANGE, Author of 'The Village of Palaces,' 'The Friendships of Mary Russell Mitford,' &c. 2 vols. crown 8vo. With Illustrations. 21s.

"Under the title of 'The Palace and the Hospital,' Mr. L'Estrange has provided for those who have a taste for topography, or rather for the historical and biographical annals of a locality famous in history, two volumes which are rich in romantic interest, and his pages abound in curious and interesting glimpses of old manners."—*Daily News.*

"Mr. L'Estrange's volumes will well repay perusal, and readers who may not be well versed in English history will gather from them information, agreeably told, as to many matters besides Greenwich Palace Hospital."—*Queen.*

FOOTSTEPS OF JEANNE D'ARC. A Pilgrimage. By Mrs. FLORENCE CADDY. 1 vol. demy 8vo. With Map of Route. 15s.

"The reader, whatever his preconceived notions of the maid may have been, will soon find himself in sympathy with a writer who, by the charm of her descriptive style, at once arrests his attention and sustains the interest of her subject."—*Morning Post.*

MESSRS. HURST AND BLACKETT'S
NEW WORKS—*Continued.*

THE LIFE AND ADVENTURES OF PEG
WOFFINGTON: WITH PICTURES OF THE PERIOD IN WHICH SHE LIVED. By J. FITZGERALD MOLLOY, Author of "Court Life Below Stairs," &c. *Second Edition.* 2 vols. crown 8vo. With Portrait. 21s.

"Peg Woffington makes a most interesting central figure, round which Mr. Molloy has made to revolve a varied and picturesque panorama of London life in the middle of the eighteenth century. He sees things in the past so clearly, grasps them so tenaciously, and reproduces them so vividly, that they come to us without any of the dust and rust of time."—G. A. S. *in Illustrated London News.*

WOMEN OF EUROPE IN THE FIFTEENTH
AND SIXTEENTH CENTURIES. By Mrs. NAPIER HIGGINS. Vols. 1 and 2 demy 8vo. 30s.

"These volumes contain biographies of women more or less directly connected with the history of Scandinavia, Germany, Hungary, Russia, Lithuania, and Poland, during the fifteenth and sixteenth centuries. The work is likely to be of permanent value to the students of history."—*Morning Post.*

ON THE TRACK OF THE CRESCENT: ERRATIC
NOTES FROM THE PIRÆUS TO PESTH. By MAJOR E. C. JOHNSON, M.A.I., F. R. Hist. S., etc. With Map and Upwards of 50 Illustrations by the Author. 1 vol. demy 8vo. 15s.

"The author of this bright, pleasant volume possesses keen power of observation and vivid appreciation of animate and inanimate beauty. It will brighten hours for many readers who will only follow the track of the Crescent through its pages and its numerous illustrations."—*Morning Post.*

MEMOIRS OF MARSHAL BUGEAUD, FROM
HIS PRIVATE CORRESPONDENCE AND ORIGINAL DOCUMENTS, 1784—1849. By the COUNT H. D'IDEVILLE. Edited, from the French, by CHARLOTTE M. YONGE. 2 vols. demy 8vo. 30s.

"This is a work of great value to the student of French history. A perusal of the book will convince any reader of Bugeaud's energy, his patriotism, his unselfishness, and his philanthropy and humanity He was, indeed, a general who may serve as a pattern to all countries, and his name deserves to live long in the memory of his countrymen."—*Athenæum.*

GLIMPSES OF GREEK LIFE AND SCENERY.
By AGNES SMITH, Author of "Eastern Pilgrims," &c. Demy 8vo. With Illustrations and Map of the Author's Route. 15s.

"A truthful picture of the country through which the author travelled. It is naturally and simply told, in an agreeable and animated style. Miss Smith displays an ample acquaintance and sympathy with all the scenes of historic interest, and is able to tell her readers a good deal of the present condition and prospects of the people who inhabit the country."—*St. James's Gazette.*

MONSIEUR GUIZOT IN PRIVATE LIFE (1787-
1874). By His Daughter, Madame DE WITT. Translated by Mrs. SIMPSON. 1 vol. demy 8vo. 15s.

"Madame de Witt has done justice to her father's memory in an admirable record of his life. Mrs. Simpson's translation of this singularly interesting book is in accuracy and grace worthy of the original and of the subject."—*Saturday Review.*

WORDS OF HOPE AND COMFORT TO
THOSE IN SORROW. Dedicated by Permission to THE QUEEN. *Fourth Edition.* 1 vol. small 4to. 5s.

DONOVAN:

A MODERN ENGLISHMAN.

"This is a very admirable work. The reader is from the first carried away by the gallant unconventionality of its author. 'Donovan' is a very excellent novel; but it is something more and better. It should do as much good as the best sermon ever written or delivered extempore. The story is told with a grand simplicity, an unconscious poetry of eloquence which stirs the very depths of the heart. One of the main excellencies of this novel is the delicacy of touch with which the author shows her most delightful characters to be after all human beings, and not angels before their time."—*Standard.*

"'Donovan' is told with the power of truth, experience, and moral insight. The tone of the novel is excellent and very high."—*Daily News.*

WE TWO.

"This book is well written and full of interest. The story abounds with a good many light touches, and is certainly far from lacking in incident."—*Times.*

"'We Two' contains many very exciting passages and a great deal of information. Miss Lyall is a capable writer and a clear-headed thinker."—*Athenæum.*

"A work of deep thought and much power. Serious as it is, it is now and then brightened by rays of genuine humour. Altogether this story is more and better than a novel."—*Morning Post.*

"There is artistic realism both in the conception and the delineation of the personages; the action and interest are unflaggingly sustained from first to last, and the book is pervaded by an atmosphere of elevated, earnest thought."—*Scotsman.*

IN THE GOLDEN DAYS.

"Miss Lyall has given us a vigorous study of such life and character as are really worth reading about. The central figure of her story is Algernon Sydney; and this figure she invests with a singular dignity and power. He always appears with effect, but no liberties are taken with the facts of his life. The plot is adapted with great felicity to them. His part in it, absolutely consistent as it is with historical truth, gives it reality as well as dignity. Some of the scenes are remarkably vivid. The escape is an admirable narrative, which almost makes one hold one's breath as one reads."—*Spectator.*

"'In the Golden Days' is an excellent novel of a kind we are always particularly glad to recommend. It has a good foundation of plot and incident, a thoroughly noble and wholesome motive, a hero who really acts and suffers heroically, and two very nice heroines. The historical background is very carefully indicated, but is never allowed to become more than background."—*Guardian.*

WON BY WAITING.

"The Dean's daughters are perfectly real characters—the learned Cornelia especially; —the little impulsive French heroine, who endures their cold hospitality and at last wins their affection, is thoroughly charming; while throughout the book there runs a golden thread of pure brotherly and sisterly love, which pleasantly reminds us that the making and marring of marriage is not, after all, the sum total of real life."—*Academy.*

"'Won by Waiting' is a very pleasing and well-written tale; full of graphic descriptions of French and English life, with incidents and characters well sustained. A book with such pleasant reading, and with such a healthy tone and influence, is a great boon to the young people in our families."—*Freeman.*

SIX-SHILLING NOVELS

EACH IN ONE VOLUME CROWN 8vo.

THE BRANDRETHS.
By the Right Hon. A. J. B. Beresford Hope, M.P.

"In 'The Brandreths' we have a sequel to Mr. Beresford Hope's clever novel of 'Strictly Tied Up,' and we may add that it is a decided improvement on his maiden effort. Mr. Hope writes of political life and the vicissitudes of parties with the knowledge and experience of a veteran politician."—*Times.*

"The great attraction of the novel is the easy, conversational, knowledgeable tone of it; the sketching from the life, and yet not so close to the life as to be malicious, men, women, periods, and events, to all of which intelligent readers can fit a name. The political and social sketches will naturally excite the chief interest among readers who will be attracted by the author's name and experience."—*Spectator.*

SOPHY.
By Violet Fane.

"'Sophy' is the clever and original work of a clever woman. Its merits are of a strikingly unusual kind. It is charged throughout with the strongest human interest. It is, in a word, a novel that will make its mark."—*World.*

"This novel is as amusing, piquant, droll, and suggestive as it can be. It overflows with humour, nor are there wanting touches of genuine feeling. To considerable imaginative power, the writer joins keen observation."—*Daily News.*

"'Sophy' throughout displays accurate knowledge of widely differing forms of character, and remarkable breadth of view. It is one of the few current novels that may not impossibly stand the test of time."—*Graphic.*

MY LORD AND MY LADY.
By Mrs. Forrester.

"This novel will take a high place among the successes of the season. It is as fresh a novel as it is interesting, as attractive as it is realistically true, as full of novelty of presentment as it is of close study and observation of life."—*World.*

"A very capital novel. The great charm about it is that Mrs. Forrester is quite at home in the society which she describes. It is a book to read."—*Standard.*

"Mrs. Forrester's style is so fresh and graphic that the reader is kept under its spell from first to last."—*Morning Post.*

HIS LITTLE MOTHER.
By the Author of "John Halifax, Gentleman."

"The author of 'John Halifax' always writes with grace and feeling, and never more so than in the present volume."—*Morning Post.*

"'His Little Mother' is one of those pathetic stories which the author tells better than anybody else."—*John Bull.*

"This book is written with all Mrs. Craik's grace of style, the chief charm of which, after all, is its simplicity."—*Glasgow Herald.*

LONDON : HURST AND BLACKETT, PUBLISHERS.

THE NEW AND POPULAR NOVELS.
PUBLISHED BY HURST & BLACKETT.

IN LETTERS OF GOLD. By THOMAS ST. E. HAKE. 2 vols.

"Mr. Hake does not indulge in padding, and never forgets that his first, and, indeed, only business, is to tell a story."—*Athenæum.*

LIKE LUCIFER. By DENZIL VANE. 3 vols.

"There is some pleasant writing in 'Like Lucifer,' and the plot is workman-like."—*Academy.*

"Denzil Vane has a talent for lively, fluent writing, and a power of tracing character."—*Whitehall Review.*

A DAUGHTER OF THE GODS. By JANE STANLEY. 2 vols.

"'A Daughter of the Gods' is very pretty. That is a description which specially suits the easy-flowing, love-making story."—*Athenæum.*

THRO' LOVE AND WAR. By VIOLET FANE, Author of "Sophy: or the Adventures of a Savage," &c. 3 vols.

"'Thro' Love and War' has a succinct and intelligible plot, and is written with a quaint combination of acute perception, veiled sarcasm, and broad fun, which is certain to ensure for it a wide popularity."—*The World.*

"We find, as we might expect from Miss Fane's past work, these three volumes brimful of cynical and racy humour, yet not lacking in serious foundation."—*Times.*

SIR ROBERT SHIRLEY, BART. By JOHN BERWICK HARWOOD, Author of "Lady Flavia," "The Tenth Earl," &c. 3 vols.

"'Sir Robert Shirley, Bart,' is a thoroughly good story. The book is wholesome in tone, and will please all those whose taste is not perverted by a too highly-spiced style of fiction."—*Morning Post.*

LUCIA. By Mrs. AUGUSTUS CRAVEN, Author of "A Sister's Story." Translated by LADY HERBERT OF LEA. 2 vols.

"This is a very pretty, touching, and consoling story. The tale is as much above the ordinary romance as the fresh air of the seaside is better than the stifling atmosphere of the fashionable quarter of the gayest city."—*St. James's Gazette.*

"'Lucia' is as good a novel as has been published for a long time."—*Academy.*

LOVE, THE PILGRIM. By MAY CROMMELIN, Author of "Queenie," "A Jewel of a Girl," &c. 3 vols.

"'Love, the Pilgrim' is a pretty story, which, beginning quietly, develops into one of very sensational incident indeed."—*Graphic.*

"A tale of thrilling interest."—*Scotsman.*

THE KING CAN DO NO WRONG. By PAMELA SNEYD, Author of "Jack Urquhart's Daughter." 2 vols.

"This novel gives evidence of imagination, insight into character, and power of delineation."—*Athenæum.*

"Shows command of exceptional narrative and descriptive power—the story is told with cleverness and force."—*Scotsman*

THE NEW AND POPULAR NOVELS.
PUBLISHED BY HURST & BLACKETT.

ONCE AGAIN. By Mrs. FORRESTER, Author of
"Viva," "Mignon," "My Lord and My Lady," &c. 3 vols.

A WILFUL YOUNG WOMAN. By A. PRICE,
Author of "A Rustic Maid," "Who is Sylvia?" &c. 3 vols.

THE SURVIVORS. By HENRY CRESSWELL, Author
of "A Modern Greek Heroine," "Incognita," &c. 3 vols.

A WICKED GIRL. By MARY CECIL HAY, Author
of "Old Myddelton's Money," &c. 3 vols.
"The Story, 'A Wicked Girl,' has a ingeniously carried out plot. Miss Hay is
a graceful writer, and her pathos is genuine."—*Morning Post.*

OUT OF THE GLOAMING. By E. J. PORTER.
2 vols.

THE WOOING OF CATHERINE. By E. FRANCES
POYNTER, Author of "My Little Lady," &c. 2 vols.
"Miss Poynter's two volumes are well-written and gracefully composed."—
Academy.

ST. BRIAVELS. By MARY DEANE, Author of
"Quatrefoil," &c. 3 vols.
"The authoress throughout writes with moderation and consistency, and her
three ample volumes well repay perusal."—*Daily Telegraph.*
"'St. Briavels' is a story replete with variety, and in all develcpments of her
plot the author skilfully maintains an unabated interest."—*Morning Post.*

THE COURTING OF MARY SMITH. By F. W.
ROBINSON, Author of "Grandmother's Money," "No Church," &c.
3 vols.
"One of the finest studies that any of our novelists has produced of late years.
To read such a book is to strengthen the soul with a moral tonic."—*Athenæum.*

A LILY MAID. By WILLIAM GEORGE WATERS.
3 vols.
"A story of the keenest interest. Mr. Waters' plot is neat, and his style is
bright and pleasing."—*Daily Telegraph.*
"'A Lily Maid' is throughout exceedingly pleasant reading."—*Morning Post.*

THE POWER OF GOLD. By GEORGE LAMBERT.
2 vols.
"'The Power of Gold' is distinguished for skill in giving fresh interest to a
simple story, and the presentation of characters with real life about them."—
Graphic.

THE BETRAYAL OF REUBEN HOLT. By
BARBARA LAKE. 1 vol. crown 8vo. 6s.
"The novel, though slight in construction, has one very dramatic episode, and
this is well worked up to."—*Publishers' Circular.*

HURST & BLACKETT'S

STANDARD LIBRARY.

HURST & BLACKETT'S STANDARD LIBRARY
OF CHEAP EDITIONS OF
POPULAR MODERN WORKS.
ILLUSTRATED BY
Sir J. E. Millais, Sir J. Gilbert, Holman Hunt, Birket Foster, John Leech, John Tenniel, J. Laslett Pott, etc.

Each in a Single Volume, with Frontispiece, price 5s.

I.—SAM SLICK'S NATURE AND HUMAN NATURE.

"The first volume of Messrs. Hurst and Blackett's Standard Library of Cheap Editions forms a very good beginning to what will doubtless be a very successful undertaking 'Nature and Human Nature' is one of the best of Sam Slick's witty and humorous productions, and well entitled to the large circulation which it cannot fail to obtain in its present convenient and cheap shape. The volume combines with the great recommendations of a clear, bold type and good paper, the lesser, but attractive merits of being well illustrated and elegantly bound."—*Morning Post.*

II.—JOHN HALIFAX, GENTLEMAN.

"The new and cheaper edition of this interesting work will doubtless meet with great success. John Halifax, the hero of this most beautiful story, is no ordinary hero, and this his history is no ordinary book. It is a full-length portrait of a true gentleman, one of nature's own nobility. It is also the history of a home, and a thoroughly English one. The work abounds in incident, and many of the scenes are full of graphic power and true pathos. It is a book that few will read without becoming wiser and better."—*Scotsman.*

"This story is very interesting. The attachment between John Halifax and his wife is beautifully painted, as are the pictures of their domestic life, and the growing up of their children; and the conclusion of the book is beautiful and touching."—*Athenæum.*

III.—THE CRESCENT AND THE CROSS.
BY ELIOT WARBURTON.

"Independent of its value as an original narrative, and its useful and interesting information, this work is remarkable for the colouring power and play of fancy with which its descriptions are enlivened. Among its greatest and most lasting charms is its reverent and serious spirit."—*Quarterly Review.*

"Mr. Warburton has fulfilled the promise of his title-page. The 'Realities of Eastern Travel' are described with a vividness which invests them with deep and abiding interest; while the 'Romantic' adventures which the enterprising tourist met with in his course are narrated with a spirit which shows how much he enjoyed these reliefs from the ennui of every-day life."—*Globe.*

IV.—NATHALIE.
BY JULIA KAVANAGH.

"'Nathalie' is Miss Kavanagh's best imaginative effort. Its manner is gracious and attractive. Its matter is good. A sentiment, a tenderness, are commanded by her which are as individual as they are elegant. We should not soon come to an end were we to specify all the delicate touches and attractive pictures which place 'Nathalie' high among books of its class."—*Athenæum.*

V.—A WOMAN'S THOUGHTS ABOUT WOMEN.
BY THE AUTHOR OF "JOHN HALIFAX, GENTLEMAN."

"These thoughts are good and humane. They are thoughts we would wish women to think: they are much more to the purpose than the treatises upon the women and daughters of England, which were fashionable some years ago, and these thoughts mark the progress of opinion, and indicate a higher tone of character, and a juster estimate of woman's position."—*Athenæum.*

"This excellent book is characterised by good sense, good taste, and feeling, and is written in an earnest, philanthropic, as well as practical spirit."—*Morning Post.*

HURST & BLACKETT'S STANDARD LIBRARY

XI.—MARGARET AND HER BRIDESMAIDS.

BY THE AUTHOR OF "THE VALLEY OF A HUNDRED FIRES."

"We recommend all who are in search of a fascinating novel to read this work for themselves. They will find it well worth their while. There are a freshness and originality about it quite charming, and there is a certain nobleness in the treatment both of sentiment and incident which is not often found."—*Athenæum.*

XII.—THE OLD JUDGE; OR, LIFE IN A COLONY.

BY SAM SLICK.

"A peculiar interest attaches to sketches of colonial life, and readers could not have a safer guide than the talented author of this work, who, by a residence of half a century, has practically grasped the habits, manners, and social conditions of the colonists he describes. All who wish to form a fair idea of the difficulties and pleasures of life in a new country, unlike England in some respects, yet like it in many, should read this book."—*John Bull.*

XIII.—DARIEN; OR, THE MERCHANT PRINCE.

BY ELIOT WARBURTON.

"This last production of the author of 'The Crescent and the Cross' has the same elements of a very wide popularity. It will please its thousands."—*Globe.*

"Eliot Warburton's active and productive genius is amply exemplified in the present book. We have seldom met with any work in which the realities of history and the poetry of fiction were more happily interwoven."—*Illustrated News.*

XIV.—FAMILY ROMANCE; OR, DOMESTIC ANNALS OF THE ARISTOCRACY.

BY SIR BERNARD BURKE, ULSTER KING OF ARMS.

"It were impossible to praise too highly this most interesting book, whether we should have regard to its excellent plan or its not less excellent execution. It ought to be found on every drawing-room table. Here you have nearly fifty captivating romances with the pith of all their interest preserved in undiminished poignancy, and any one may be read in half an hour. It is not the least of their merits that the romances are founded on fact —or what, at least, has been handed down for truth by long tradition—and the romance of reality far exceeds the romance of fiction."—*Standard.*

XV.—THE LAIRD OF NORLAW.

BY MRS. OLIPHANT.

"We have had frequent opportunities of commending Messrs. Hurst and Blackett's Standard Library. For neatness, elegance, and distinctness the volumes in this series surpass anything with which we are familiar. 'The Laird of Norlaw' will fully sustain the author's high reputation. The reader is carried on from first to last with an energy of sympathy that never flags."—*Sunday Times.*

"'The Laird of Norlaw' is worthy of the author's reputation. It is one of the most exquisite of modern novels."—*Observer.*

XVI.—THE ENGLISHWOMAN IN ITALY.

BY MRS. G. GRETTON.

"Mrs. Gretton had opportunities which rarely fall to the lot of strangers of becoming acquainted with the inner life and habits of a part of the Italian peninsula which is the very centre of the national crisis. We can praise her performance as interesting, unexaggerated, and full of opportune instruction."—*The Times.*

"Mrs. Gretton's book is timely, life-like, and for every reason to be recommended. It is impossible to close the book without liking the writer as well as the subject. The work is engaging, because real."—*Athenæum.*

HURST & BLACKETT'S STANDARD LIBRARY

XVII.—NOTHING NEW.

BY THE AUTHOR OF "JOHN HALIFAX, GENTLEMAN."

"'Nothing New' displays all those superior merits which have made 'John Halifax' one of the most popular works of the day. There is a force and truthfulness about these tales which mark them as the production of no ordinary mind, and we cordially recommend them to the perusal of all lovers of fiction."—*Morning Post.*

XVIII.—LIFE OF JEANNE D'ALBRET, QUEEN OF NAVARRE.

BY MISS FREER.

"We have read this book with great pleasure, and have no hesitation in recommending it to general perusal. It reflects the highest credit on the industry and ability of Miss Freer. Nothing can be more interesting than her story of the life of Jeanne D'Albret, and the narrative is as trustworthy as it is attractive."—*Morning Post.*

XIX.—THE VALLEY OF A HUNDRED FIRES.

BY THE AUTHOR OF "MARGARET AND HER BRIDESMAIDS."

"If asked to classify this work, we should give it a place between 'John Halifax' and 'The Caxtons.'"—*Standard.*

"The spirit in which the whole book is written is refined and good."—*Athenæum.*

"This is in every sense a charming novel."—*Messenger.*

XX.—THE ROMANCE OF THE FORUM; OR, NARRATIVES, SCENES, AND ANECDOTES FROM COURTS OF JUSTICE.

BY PETER BURKE, SERJEANT AT LAW.

"This attractive book will be perused with much interest. It contains a great variety of singular and highly romantic stories."—*John Bull.*

"A work of singular interest, which can never fail to charm and absorb the reader's attention. The present cheap and elegant edition includes the true story of the Colleen Bawn."—*Illustrated News.*

XXI.—ADÈLE.

BY JULIA KAVANAGH.

"'Adèle' is the best work we have read by Miss Kavanagh; it is a charming story, full of delicate character-painting. The interest kindled in the first chapter burns brightly to the close."—*Athenæum.*

"'Adèle' will fully sustain the reputation of Miss Kavanagh, high as it already ranks."—*John Bull.*

"'Adèle' is a love-story of very considerable pathos and power. It is a very clever novel."—*Daily News.*

XXII.—STUDIES FROM LIFE.

BY THE AUTHOR OF "JOHN HALIFAX, GENTLEMAN."

"These 'Studies' are truthful and vivid pictures of life, often earnest, always full of right feeling, and occasionally lightened by touches of quiet, genial humour. The volume is remarkable for thought, sound sense, shrewd observation, and kind and sympathetic feeling for all things good and beautiful."—*Morning Post.*

"These 'Studies from Life' are remarkable for graphic power and observation. The book will not diminish the reputation of the accomplished author."—*Saturday Review.*

HURST & BLACKETT'S STANDARD LIBRARY

XXIII.—GRANDMOTHER'S MONEY.

BY F. W. ROBINSON.

"We commend 'Grandmother's Money' to readers in search of a good novel. The characters are true to human nature, and the story is interesting."—*Athenæum.*

XXIV.—A BOOK ABOUT DOCTORS.

BY JOHN CORDY JEAFFRESON.

"A book to be read and re-read; fit for the study as well as the drawing-room table and the circulating library."—*Lancet.*

"This is a pleasant book for the fireside season, and for the seaside season. Mr. Jeaffreson has, out of hundreds of volumes, collected thousands of good things, adding thereto much that appears in print for the first time, and which, of course, gives increased value to this very readable book."—*Athenæum.*

XXV.—NO CHURCH.

BY F. W. ROBINSON.

"We advise all who have the opportunity to read this book. It is well worth the study."—*Athenæum.*

"A work of great originality, merit, and power."—*Standard.*

XXVI.—MISTRESS AND MAID.

BY THE AUTHOR OF "JOHN HALIFAX, GENTLEMAN."

"A good wholesome book, gracefully written, and as pleasant to read as it is instructive."—*Athenæum.*

"A charming tale, charmingly told."—*Standard.*

"All lovers of a good novel will hail with delight another of Mrs. Craik's charming stories."—*John Bull.*

XXVII.—LOST AND SAVED.

BY THE HON. MRS. NORTON.

"'Lost and Saved' will be read with eager interest by those who love a touching story. It is a vigorous novel."—*Times.*

"This story is animated, full of exciting situations and stirring incidents. The characters are delineated with great power. Above and beyond these elements of a good novel, there is that indefinable charm with which true genius invests all it touches."—*Daily News.*

XXVIII.—LES MISERABLES.

BY VICTOR HUGO.

Authorised Copyright English Translation.

"The merits of 'Les Miserables' do not merely consist in the conception of it as a whole; it abounds with details of unequalled beauty. M. Victor Hugo has stamped upon every page the hall-mark of genius."—*Quarterly Review.*

XXIX.—BARBARA'S HISTORY.

BY AMELIA B. EDWARDS.

"It is not often that we light upon a novel of so much merit and interest as 'Barbara's History.' It is a work conspicuous for taste and literary culture. It is a very graceful and charming book, with a well-managed story, clearly-cut characters, and sentiments expressed with an exquisite elocution. The dialogues especially sparkle with repartee. It is a book which the world will like. This is high praise of a work of art and so we intend it."—*The Times.*

HURST & BLACKETT'S STANDARD LIBRARY

XXXVIII.—ROBERT FALCONER.

BY GEORGE MAC DONALD, LL.D.

"'Robert Falconer' is a work brimful of life and humour and of the deepest human interest. It is a book to be returned to again and again for the deep and searching knowledge it evinces of human thoughts and feelings."—*Athenæum.*

XXXIX.—THE WOMAN'S KINGDOM.

BY THE AUTHOR OF "JOHN HALIFAX, GENTLEMAN."

"'The Woman's Kingdom' sustains the author's reputation as a writer of the purest and noblest kind of domestic stories."—*Athenæum.*

"'The Woman's Kingdom' is remarkable for its romantic interest. The characters are masterpieces. Edna is worthy of the hand that drew John Halifax."—*Morning Post.*

XL.—ANNALS OF AN EVENTFUL LIFE.

BY GEORGE WEBBE DASENT, D.C.L.

"A racy, well-written, and original novel. The interest never flags. The whole work sparkles with wit and humour."—*Quarterly Review.*

XLI.—DAVID ELGINBROD.

BY GEORGE MAC DONALD, LL.D.

"A novel which is the work of a man of genius. It will attract the highest class of readers."—*Times.*

XLII.—A BRAVE LADY.

BY THE AUTHOR OF "JOHN HALIFAX, GENTLEMAN."

"We earnestly recommend this novel. It is a special and worthy specimen of the author's remarkable powers. The reader's attention never for a moment flags."—*Post*

"'A Brave Lady' thoroughly rivets the unmingled sympathy of the reader, and her history deserves to stand foremost among the author's works."—*Daily Telegraph.*

XLIII.—HANNAH.

BY THE AUTHOR OF "JOHN HALIFAX, GENTLEMAN."

"A very pleasant, healthy story, well and artistically told. The book is sure of a wide circle of readers. The character of Hannah is one of rare beauty."—*Standard.*

"A powerful novel of social and domestic life. One of the most successful efforts of a successful novelist."—*Daily News.*

XLIV.—SAM SLICK'S AMERICANS AT HOME.

"This is one of the most amusing books that we ever read."—*Standard.*

"'The Americans at Home' will not be less popular than any of Judge Halliburton's previous works."—*Morning Post.*

XLV.—THE UNKIND WORD.

BY THE AUTHOR OF "JOHN HALIFAX, GENTLEMAN."

"These stories are gems of narrative. Indeed, some of them, in their touching grace and simplicity, seem to us to possess a charm even beyond the authoress's most popular novels. Of none of them can this be said more emphatically than of that which opens the series, 'The Unkind Word.' It is wonderful to see the imaginative power displayed in the few delicate touches by which this successful love-story is sketched out."—*The Echo.*

XLVI.—A ROSE IN JUNE.

BY MRS. OLIPHANT.

"'A Rose in June' is as pretty as its title. The story is one of the best and most touching which we owe to the industry and talent of Mrs. Oliphant, and may hold its own with even 'The Chronicles of Carlingford.'"—*Times.*

XLVII.—MY LITTLE LADY.

BY E. FRANCES POYNTER.

"This story presents a number of vivid and very charming pictures. Indeed, the whole book is charming. It is interesting in both character and story, and thoroughly good of its kind."—*Saturday Review.*

XLVIII.—PHŒBE, JUNIOR.

BY MRS. OLIPHANT.

"This last 'Chronicle of Carlingford' not merely takes rank fairly beside the first which introduced us to 'Salem Chapel,' but surpasses all the intermediate records. Phœbe, Junior, herself is admirably drawn."—*Academy.*

XLIX.—LIFE OF MARIE ANTOINETTE.

BY PROFESSOR CHARLES DUKE YONGE.

"A work of remarkable merit and interest, which will, we doubt not, become the most popular English history of Marie Antoinette."—*Spectator.*

L.—SIR GIBBIE.

BY GEORGE MAC DONALD, LL.D.

"'Sir Gibbie' is a book of genius."—*Pall Mall Gazette.*
"This book has power, pathos, and humour."—*Athenæum.*

LI.—YOUNG MRS. JARDINE.

BY THE AUTHOR OF "JOHN HALIFAX, GENTLEMAN."

"'Young Mrs. Jardine' is a pretty story, written in pure English."—*The Times.*
"There is much good feeling in this book. It is pleasant and wholesome."—*Athenæum.*

LII.—LORD BRACKENBURY.

BY AMELIA B. EDWARDS.

"A very readable story. The author has well conceived the purpose of high-class novel-writing, and succeeded in no small measure in attaining it. There is plenty of variety, cheerful dialogue, and general 'verve' in the book."—*Athenæum.*

LIII.—IT WAS A LOVER AND HIS LASS.

BY MRS. OLIPHANT.

"In 'It was a Lover and his Lass,' we admire Mrs. Oliphant exceedingly. It would be worth reading a second time, were it only for the sake of one ancient Scottish spinster, who is nearly the counterpart of the admirable Mrs. Margaret Maitland."—*Times.*

LIV.—THE REAL LORD BYRON—THE STORY OF THE POET'S LIFE.

BY JOHN CORDY JEAFFRESON.

"Mr. Jeaffreson comes forward with a narrative which must take a very important place in Byronic literature; and it may reasonably be anticipated that this book will be regarded with deep interest by all who are concerned in the works and the fame of this great English poet."—*The Times.*